Join my New Releases and Sales newsletter at: http://eepurl.com/beV0gf

Author's note: I also write romantic comedy as Julia Kent and paranormal shifter romance as one-half of the writing duo Diana Seere. Check out those books as well. ;)

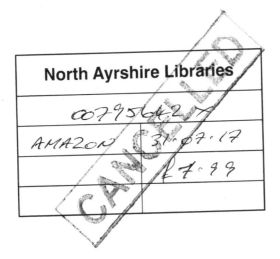

CHAPTER ONE

There's a gun in my ribs, right above my hipbone, and Mark Paulson smells like metal and death.

It's a beautiful Southern California day, with not a cloud in the sky. The air smells like salt and sweet freedom. Freshly-mowed grass tickles my nose as a light breeze sweeps past, just a passing fancy, an airborne visitor.

This is Hollywood perfect. We could be on a movie set. But we're not.

"Lindsay," he says, his face hidden by my proximity to him, his arm holding me close, as if he's protecting me as he escorts me to the stairs to board the helicopter.

But if he's protecting me, why is he holding me at gunpoint?

What the hell?

That's *not* Mark.

My world pinpoints. I can't see his face, but that's not his voice. I know that voice.

I'd know it anywhere.

John Gainsborough.

I look back at Anya, who just walked me out to the landing strip, leaving me at the halfway point. Like the good little girl that I am, I followed. They've trained me well, right? Besides, I'm surrounded by my security detail. What am I supposed to do – disobey?

Certainly not now.

My knees buckle. His grasp is hard, holding me up, not caring that my high heel snaps, my feet an afterthought. I try to look over to the building, the helicopter blades slicing through sound itself, taking over.

I'm about to faint.

No. I can't faint.

Drew, I want to scream. *Where are you?*

"Get in," John says in a pleasant voice, as if we're taking a day jaunt to a private island. As if we're off for a pleasant sun-filled trip with yachts and jet-skis, cavalier and free, troubled only by our own stresses and worries about not conforming to the expectations set by our peers and parents.

If only.

I can't scream, because the sound of the helicopter blades takes over all the available space for noise. Nothing I do will get anyone's attention.

How's that for irony? The whole point of coming home was to blend into the scenery and be a boring prop for Daddy's family image.

And now I can't make myself stand out long enough to be saved.

Daddy said I was going back to the Island. Even he couldn't lie to me and pretend his coffee plantation plan was real. Gentle yet firm, he'd sat me down last night to explain it all.

And I'd complied, because good girls do what they're asked, right?

All the while, I'd rubbed my hands together, worrying that little Band-aid next to my thumb.

Nothing they do matters.

Nothing.

Not Daddy, not Stellan, Blaine and John, not my mother – no one.

Because Drew's smarter than all of them.

And he's coming for me.

No matter what.

That thought comforts me as John shoves me, hard, up into the helicopter. My shin bangs against the iron step, the metal's edge scraping up the long, thin bone so hard I know it'll leave a speckled bruise in the morning.

He's strong, with tight muscles. That's right. Baseball player. John Gainsborough, big league pitcher extraordinaire. Top of his game, and in prime condition. A guy like that has some serious discipline, right?

I should scream. Pain sears me, his scent a swift reminder of the past, John's musk drifting into my nose.

I'm transported back four years.

Only this time, I know what he's about to do.

What *they're* about to do.

I'm not sure which is worse.

Not knowing or knowing.

I go limp. I'm not making this easy for him. The longer I delay, the more time Drew has to rescue me.

"Cute," he hisses in my ear, licking the shell. Horror bursts through me, my blood carrying messages to my limbs, my brain, all screaming *danger!* as I stop breathing. My breath halts as if it can't continue.

Just *can't.*

"If you think your participation in anything, including walking, is optional, Lindsay, you're sorely mistaken. We've been waiting for you. We have quite the plan." His voice is filled with glee.

"You're so screwed," I whisper, the defiance unable to keep itself inside. My words come out in a *whoosh* as my body remembers to breathe.

"Screwed? We're all about to be screwed. And so much more." John's face splits into a grin.

When we were in high school, I had a mad crush on him. We all did. Tall and muscular, with pale gray eyes and the look of an athlete with a fine brain, he was the golden boy. The guy every girl wanted for her own.

I find him repulsive now. Being touched by him is like being caressed by an angry slug.

"Drew is coming for me." The words are out before I know it. I have made a mistake. I know I have, yet I'm emboldened by saying it. Acknowledging the truth gives me power, even as the world turns to white and black dots before my eyes. He is. I know he is, my cells screaming for him, sending signals to the man who loved me enough to

7

spend the last four years readying for this moment.

Which is unfolding without him.

"Drew?" John's laughter is bitter and nasty, condescending and so self-assured that a zing of electric fear shoots from my teeth to my ass. "Drew is in police custody for stalking you."

I sniff, then sniff again, my body's desperate attempt to get oxygen in me. My tongue is flat in my mouth, pressed hard against my bottom teeth, and my throat goes dry as sandpaper.

"Shut up, John," shouts another voice. I can barely hear him over the helicopter. They get me into a seat and quickly close the chopper's door. No one bothers to buckle me in. I close my eyes.

"Playing possum? Cute."

Why are they ruining the word *cute*?

As the helicopter lifts off, I crack one eyelid.

Stellan. Of course.

I say nothing. I can't. If I have a speech center in my brain, it's shut down so the rest of me can work on pure survival. I know from four years on the Island that the mind can be your best friend or your worst enemy. Thoughts loop through me, triggering a rush of fear so great I think it'll tear my skin into ribbons in an attempt to flee my body.

Because my body is the target.

Drew's in police custody? For stalking me? What does that all mean? He didn't stalk me.

My mind scrambles to put the pieces together.

Set up. It's a set up. Drew's being turned into the scapegoat.

Oh, God.

If they're telling the truth, how will he get out? How will he rescue me?

I can't look at them. Screaming won't make a difference. Out of the corner of my eye I see Silas outside, right by the double doors to the house. My heart squeezes in my chest. As we rise higher and higher, he gets smaller and smaller.

He failed.

He doesn't know it yet, but he failed.

DREW

I wake up on a thin blanket on the floor in a holding cell, my cheek ice cold, the throbbing in my head a bass drum. The ground beneath my body is clean. It smells like mildew and bleach. The distinct ammonia odor of piss is mixed in there.

I know this scent.

It's the smell of jail. I've spent plenty of time immersed in it in the past, but always as the jailer.

Not the *jailee*.

Gingerly, I start to sit up, inch by inch. My body is unclothed except for my boxer briefs. Shoes are gone, pants are gone, shirt is gone.

Dignity – *long* gone.

I hear the click and clack of a heavy-duty lock opening. The door to the cell moves and there stands Mark Paulson.

He's white as a sheet and his jaw is tight.

It takes me a few seconds to realize he's not mad at me.

He's in crisis mode.

"Just got off the phone with Harry Bosworth. Re-establishing a connection was hell. According to the senator, his assistant Anya was told Mark Paulson would bring the helicopter to take Lindsay back to the Island. She escorted Lindsay halfway to the helicopter, then I -- " He chokes on the word, running a furious hand through his blond hair, face exploding with rage " -- someone *impersonating me* escorted her to the copter, where they took off."

"When?"

"An hour ago."

"Sweet Jesus, I've been out cold for an hour?"

"Look, Drew, this is a fucking mess."

"This is fucking *unreal*. We need to get Lindsay

9

now!"

"You're being charged with so many federal and state crimes you'll be lucky to get out of jail when you're a mummy."

"Not funny."

"Not joking."

"What the hell are you doing to rescue her, Mark?"

"Everything we can. We're trying to track her, but the chopper turns out to be..." He gives me a bleak look.

Yeah. I can guess. It's not one of Harry's. Not government-issued, but made to look like one.

We've been had. *Badly*. Outsmarted and outmaneuvered.

"She's chipped," I blurt out, talking more to myself than him. Reassuring myself.

Because that's all I have right now. Words.

I don't give a shit about Mark's feelings right now. Losing a client is one of the worst experiences for a person whose sworn duty is to protect people. Losing my *girlfriend* turns this into a clusterfuck of emotional madness.

The look on his face when I say that gives me hope.

"You chipped her?" He grimaces as he confirms what I said. "That won't do us any good. A microchip only gives us information about her when we scan. It'll be good for identifying her body if -- "

Might as well kick me in the gut.

"It's a GPS-enabled microchip."

"Those don't exist." Mark shoots me an incredulous look. His eyes narrow as if he's rethinking my mental state.

I'd do the same if the roles were reversed.

I give him sour look. Of course they do. He should know better.

"Whoa," he hisses. "I thought we were years from that."

I don't bother to answer. My tongue licks the corner of my mouth, finding a raw split and blood.

"How do you track her?" he asks, bending down to

talk at eye level.

My skin starts to crawl with awakening. The aches and bruises will fade over time, but time is of the essence now for Lindsay. She must be terrified.

And I know she's waiting for me. I can't fail her.

I *won't*.

"Get me out of here."

"I can't! They're --"

"Get. Me. Out. Of. Here."

"For a guy who's being charged with enough offenses to stay in prison for the rest of your life, Drew, you're awfully demanding."

"And for a guy who just kidnapped my girlfriend, you're being an asshole, Mark."

His eyes widen, jaw dropping, face gobsmacked. And then he bristles.

"You know damn well that wasn't me."

"And you know damn well I didn't do any of the things I'm charged with," I reply.

"I know that!"

"Then DO SOMETHING about it! You're Mark Paulson, for fuck's sake!" I explode.

"Like what?"

"You're the famous Senator James Thornberg's grandson. According to Harry, you walk on water. Use that influence. Make calls. Get me the hell out of here so I can go get Lindsay."

"It's not that simple."

"*Make* it that simple."

"There are limits to what I can do, Drew."

"Push them all. Push every fucking limit until it breaks, then get me out of here."

"If – *if!* -- there's even the smallest chance I can get you out, it'll take days. Weeks. Give me the microchip information so I can start pinpointing Lindsay's location now."

I stare him down.

Here's the thing: I trust Mark Paulson with my life. With Lindsay's life.

But my brain feels like someone filled it with wet helium balloons. I just got the shit kicked out of me in custody after a raid on my apartment for crimes I didn't commit. "Mark Paulson" kidnapped my girlfriend from her father's high-security compound.

I don't know who to trust.

A flash of insight into Lindsay's frame of mind the day we left the Island hits me between the eyes.

Mark lets out a nasty sigh of disbelief. He knows what I'm thinking. "That wasn't *me*."

I just look at him. He's blurry on one side. I reach up to find a very raw right eye socket on my face. Pain blooms as I touch it.

"They really roughed you up," he says with sympathy, handing me a small package of baby wipes from his breast pocket. I open them and gently blot the facial injuries.

"Nothing compared to what Stellan, Blaine and John are about to do to Lindsay. They won't just kill her, Mark. You know that, right? You know." My voice rises. "You know they'll torment her like a cat with a captive mouse. They'll wring every bit of sick pleasure from torturing her, and then they'll do the worst thing imaginable."

"Kill her," he whispers.

"No. They'll force her to *live*." The idea of Lindsay in pain, wondering where I am, left to suffer by those jackals shoves my blood faster through me, making all my injuries throb. I'm a live wire with nowhere for the electricity to go.

He gives me a pained look, then his face goes blank, his long sigh the sound of determination. "I have a contact."

"Good of you to think about that now." I can hear the snarl in my voice. Don't care.

Lindsay. Oh, God, Lindsay. What are they doing to you right now?

"It's my dad."

"Your dad's dead."

"No – this is my biological father."

I squint. It hurts. "Your biological what?"

He shakes his head. "Remember Galt?"

Galt. Galt. Oh, yeah. Mark's biodad. Deep undercover CIA. Whatever they did to me involved too many blows to the head. My thoughts feel like scrambled eggs.

So do my balls.

Mark continues. "Bottom line: I'll have to go way, *way* outside the law to get you out. And if it doesn't work, we both end up in prison."

"If I can't get to Lindsay, I might as well die." I pull myself up and stretch, inventorying. My right shoulder's been wrenched hard, a tendon screaming as I rotate the joint. I taste blood no matter how many times I swallow, and I'm stripped down to underwear. I don't care.

Get me out.

The words turn into a non-stop thought that won't let go. *Getmeoutgetmeoutgetmeout.*

"I wish I could say no one's dying on my watch, Drew, but I can't."

When you spend days in a war-torn region in the desert, hours of monotony and boredom sprinkled in between minutes of terror and chaos, you learn to look at people differently. No shell. No walls. The look Mark and I exchange says thousands of words in seconds.

He's pretty sure he can't save Lindsay.

And I'm damn fucking sure I *will*.

"And I wish I could say I trust you with the GPS tracking system for Lindsay, but here's the deal, Mark – get me the fuck out of here and I'll give you that information."

"She could die in the meantime."

"She could die if the wrong people get that information. It's the only way I can save her."

"You really don't trust me."

"If the roles were reversed, would *you* trust *me*?" I wince as my eyes widen with emphasis, the skin tender and paper-thin. Compartmentalizing the pain is key now. Pretending it's not there is how I survive.

It's how I find Lindsay.

"Fuck."

He spins on his heel and slams the door shut.

Funny. I would have answered the same way, too.

CHAPTER TWO

LINDSAY

"**O**kay," I concede. "You win. Why me? Why are you doing this?" It takes so much control not to cry, or whine. The slight shake in my voice is pretty damn understandable, given the circumstances. Every muscle I have, including my lungs, keeps tightening, as if making them smaller will make me less likely to be hurt.

Not possible.

John shrugs. *Shrugs.*

"It's nothing personal."

I cough, choking on a universe-sized dose of incredulity. Nothing personal? This is *nothing personal*? A thousand responses flood my mind but I'm not rational, so none of them come out.

"Don't you have a game or something? I thought baseball players didn't get days off during the season."

He pretends his shoulder hurts, rubbing it while pursing his lips in a pretend pout. "Perfectly-timed injury," he says, adding a smile that doesn't meet his eyes. "I have three days with nothing to do." He leans in, his hand stroking my jaw. I close my eyes but don't jerk away. "I get to do *you*," he whispers, his breath filled with moisture, like he's licking my face although it's just air.

My ribs cave in on themselves, tensing so hard I'm afraid they'll crack, my belly clenching.

I can't let go. Can't relax. I start to shiver. I can't control it. My bladder threatens to let go. Suddenly, I'm ten feet away from my body, because really, what else can my caged mind do?

I'm in hell.

People do whatever it takes not to be in hell. We have a biological drive to survive. It goes beyond the body.

Speaking of the body, I remember the microchip. A whimper comes out of my nose. Tears fill the back of my throat, hot and salty, thickening. I nearly gag but control myself, a sob trying to work its way out.

If nothing else, they'll find my body. Drew's chip gives me that relief.

Unless they cut my hand off.

The helicopter cuts a sharp right, angling down, and because they didn't buckle me in, I roll into the door. John thumps against me, his hip digging into my butt. His body is tight and physically radiates heat that makes me nauseated. I can't stand having him breathing in my hair, his hands on my ribs as the helicopter rights and he pretends to need to touch me to sit up.

Why pretend? I have no power. He can do anything he wants to me right now.

The thought makes the world go wavy, white dots filling my vision.

Oh, no.

No, no, no.

I will *not* black out. I will not faint. Every one of my wits needs to be sharp, because Drew is going to find me. He will. I damn well know it. The pinch of the cut on my hand is a blessed pain. It makes me remember how much he cared, even when he wasn't sure about me. Back at Jane's place, I thought he was crazy but went along with it because he's *my* crazy. Mine.

I know I've blown hot and cold since I've been home from the Island. I had to.

Until the moment Drew cut me open and put that chip in me, I didn't know.

It's like having someone hand you their heart.

In the real world, where daughters aren't used as pawns against their politician fathers and pro baseball players don't kidnap women for sadistic pleasure, having your body invaded by an electronic microchip would be the epitome of hell, but no.

In my world?

It's the best form of love.

Drew will find me. Even if he has to break out of jail, he will.

He'll die trying.

The question is: will he *find me* first?

Or *die* first?

"Four years," John says as a blissfully welcome coolness fills the sudden pocket of air between us. He pulls away, giving me a grin that is meant to make me feel sick. "Four years we've been waiting."

"Don't you have something else in your life, John? You're a pro baseball player," I say, my voice croaking, the words coming out in halting syllables. He smells like sweat and expensive men's aftershave with a hint of fabric softener thrown in. It's too much. My stomach starts to tighten and release, the bile rising up my throat.

I'm going to puke. I can't stop it.

He grabs my hair at the back of my head and wrenches my neck, twisting me almost too far, almost enough to snap my spinal cord.

Almost.

I gag and vomit on the floor by the door, but there's not much there.

My stomach keeps heaving until I'm completely out of control, body limp and tense at the same time, my mind clawing its way out of my skull, trying to deny what's really happening to me.

I'm a human being these monsters are about to turn into a toy.

The toy stops being fun when it's dead.

Until then?

They'll extract their amusement.

And I can't stop them.

The thick black hood over my head comes as no surprise, but it has a strange scent like sweet, freshly-cut grass. The odor makes it hard for me to keep my eyes open, turning sour, like rotten fruit.

And then I'm gone.
Gone.

DREW

"Foster! Get your fucking ass up if you want out of here." The words come to me in a dream. I can't move. I'm cold, encased in ice, and my hands are bound. After Mark left, they gave me a pair of orange scrubs, flip-flops, a nasty sandwich, and then cuffed me.

Then my gut seizes as someone kicks me, hard, right above my cock.

All the air rushes into me, then out, like a vacuum cleaner hose is attached to my lips. I cough and gag, but know instinctively that I have to stand. I open my eyes. No Mark.

Where's Mark?

Wait.

I look at the cop, whose arms are crossed over his chest, a clipboard in one hand, banging against the wall as he shows his impatience in a slightly kinder way than kicking me again.

Did he say "want out of here"?

"You're free," he spits out, jaw set, impatience an odor he should patent. The cell door opens and he stands there, looking at the ceiling like it's the Sistine Chapel.

I have just enough wits not to ask anything, shuffling out of the room, taking a deep breath. Hallway air is still disgusting in a jail, but it's ten times better than cell air.

We walk down the long hallway, where someone in a suit hands me a manila envelope without a single word. It's a man with a bureaucrat's glare. He looks like no one and everyone. The human being equivalent of a beige wall.

All the hair on my body stands up straight, the pores practically seizing.

I know his type.

He's a man the government needs.

And he's a man the government doesn't want you to

know even exists.

He leans over, smooth and suave, his suit jacket flapping open and revealing a weapon as he pushes the bar on an exit door. I'm blinded by the sun. He shoves me out onto a small concrete landing attached to a set of stairs. Before I can catch my footing, my ankle turns and I'm falling.

My hands are still cuffed with a zip tie, fingers fumbling to catch purchase on the thick pipe-like railing as my ribs crack against the edge of a cement stair, then another, my kidney bashed in, my hip screaming. Tightening into a ball and putting my hands behind my head to protect the base of my neck, I wrench something in my shoulder. The *pop* is so strong throughout my bones I can feel it in my inner ear.

Can't count the stairs, but it's a full flight. My body inventories that much. I'm defenseless without separate hands, my cuffed wrists making the fall down the stairs agony.

And then I'm down, flat, paused. Sand and tar and a cigarette butt, casually tossed aside forever ago, press against my lips.

And blood, of course. I taste copper and uncertainty as I open my mouth and spit, clearing it.

I look up just as the door clicks shut, a wall of grey metal, the outline of the threshold barely visible.

I'm free.

Wherever I am, I'm free.

Mark did his job.

I have no clue where I am, though. Rolling carefully, I realize my hip won't move. It's not that I can't move it. The ability to pivot is gone. Blown out.

Not good.

Gingerly, I shift a different way, pulling myself up to a sitting position, sliding across the filthy asphalt, praying there's no broken glass. I'm injured enough. I don't need more right now.

It's going to be a long day.

Once I'm propped against the brick wall, I exhale,

willing my muscles to relax. They revolt. I try again. They give me the silent treatment.

I just breathe.

No amount of panicking is going to save Lindsay right now, but I need to act. In order to act, I need to get to a computer where I can track Lindsay's chip. To get a computer, I need Mark or Silas or someone to help me.

Where the fuck is Mark? It's dawning on me that I have to trust him. There's no choice here.

Regroup. I need to regroup. Figuring out where I am isn't as important as orienting myself. I look up at the sun. It is waning, but bright. I pull my right hand up to shield my eyes and realize I can't.

Can't move my right arm.

The muscles don't hurt. They just don't cooperate, as if there's an invisible line on the horizon and my arm can't go higher. My chest starts to spasm. My lips stick together, tongue dry and coated.

Thirst. I'm dehydrated. I'll be fine once I orient and get help. Whatever's wrong with me can't be as bad as what they're about to do to Lindsay.

I have to stop them.

Squinting, I look at the sun again. I'm facing southeast. It's about six p.m., give or take half an hour. Lindsay's been gone for how long?

Someone has shoved a balloon up my nose and into my sinus cavity and is slowly blowing it up until it pops. I close my eyes and gingerly push myself up the wall to standing.

Shake it off, *Drew*, I tell myself. *You've been through worse.*

And it's true.

I have.

Lurching like a drunk after a three-day bender, I stick to the wall, walking along the line of thick cement block, painted institutional gray. The bustle of the city is in the distance, the stench of urine and exhaust overwhelming my remaining open nostril. The last time I was this injured, I smelled ozone and dirt, sand and heat, the high temperature and blinding sun searing my nostrils.

By comparison, today is a cakewalk.

Getting out of this zip tie is paramount. Old training flashes through my mind. I pull my aching shoulders up and grab the end of the zip tie with my teeth. I tighten as much as I can, until my wrists scream. The plastic cuts my skin at the thumb joint.

I drop the manila envelope.

I lift my arms over my head, forcing my right arm up, then flare my elbows slightly as I smash my cuffed wrists into my stomach, tightening my core. As I bring my shoulder blades close together during the sharp, sudden movement, I ignore the bones screaming.

Snap!

Mission accomplished.

I grab the envelope and stagger down to the street.

At the end of this wall I'll be able to grab a cab. My good hand holds my manila envelope. My wallet's in there. I lean against the wall and pull all the items out.

My gun's gone, of course.

Cash, too.

But my credit cards and ID are in my wallet.

I hail a cab. It takes seven tries before a guy who looks worse than me pulls over, grinning with a mouth full of seven teeth, total.

"You look like shit, man. Where to?"

I've never been more grateful for an insult.

And then I give him The Grove's address.

Because, really, how much worse can this day get?

CHAPTER THREE

LINDSAY

Losing long chunks of time while you're unconscious normally involves the added benefit of dreams. As someone's rough hands slip my pants off over my hips, I wake up, my face itchy from rubbing against warm, wet cloth. My nose screams with a strange buzzing that makes me want to scratch all the flesh off and douse it with paint thinner.

All the skin along my inner thighs tightens painfully, as if I expect these hands to shove my legs open and pierce me. All that actually happens is that the black cloth bag stays on my head while my body is stripped of every stitch of clothing. Someone puts me in a skin-tight series of clothes, like a bodice with thick leggings and panties. The searing shame ripples on my skin like an extinction burst.

I can't control my body's responses. If I keep reacting, though, I'll lose energy. Focus. The ability to think and strategize.

All I can do is deaden my emotions. Reduce my reactions.

Go *numb*.

The less I react, the better. The less I do to draw attention to myself, the less likely I'll suffer abuse.

I know it's foolish to hope.

But hope and Drew are all I've got.

And Drew's not here.

I don't know exactly what my captors are doing. I try to be as limp as possible, pretending to still be unconscious. This won't save me. I know.

But it's the best I can come up with under the circumstances.

My mouth is dry and sour, tasting gross. I flash back to being bound, waking up with Jane over me, crying and babbling. Four years ago, I was just a body they played with.

And here I am again.

Where are you, Drew?

I slow down my breathing and try to take in my surroundings with my ears. The ocean laps in the distance, gentle sounds interspersed with crashing waves. The Island.

I must really be on the Island.

I inhale slowly, deliberately, as quietly as possible. On the Island, the constant start and stop of golf carts on the grounds was like a sitcom laugh track, punctuating the rhythm of the days.

No golf cart hum.

On the Island, helicopters came and went at least twice a day. So far, no helicopter other than ours.

And on the Island, ice cream trucks didn't exist. The tinkle of a truck's melody announcing its presence to kids and ice-cream-hungry adults shatters my theory.

No.

Not the Island.

My heart races as I take in the scent. It's nothing like the Island, inside or out. All of the buildings there had an institutional, bleach-like scent. And outdoors was filled with salty ocean air.

This smells like someone's home.

Oh, God, please don't tell me I'm at John's house.

"Sleeping Beauty awakens," says a new voice, not John's. It doesn't sound like Blaine, who is California cool, inside and out, born and bred.

Must be Stellan.

How does he know I'm awake?

Before I can react, the hood comes off and I spasm out in a coughing fit.

"Hello, Lindsay." I can't close my eyes fast enough.

It's Stellan.

I say nothing.

He nudges me with his toe. "You're being rude. You won't like what we do to rude little girls."

My jaw tightens. I couldn't talk if I wanted to. I imagine Drew pulling Stellan away from me and punching him. My neck releases slightly at the image.

Time.

Time is my friend. The longer I can buy time, the better the chance Drew can get me before they, well...

Before they kill me.

A hopeless black hole takes over at my core. It expands, like a pupil dilating, taking over my bones, my organs, my flesh, my everything.

I'm about to be hurt badly.

Tortured.

Violated.

And I can't stop it. Being drugged would be preferable to this. Maybe later, I'll beg for that.

I can try to lessen the severity. But Drew's not coming anytime soon.

I freeze. My stomach feels heavy and painful, turning and twisting until I start to retch again.

"You puke on me and I crack open your eye socket," Stellan says calmly, not making eye contact. "Again."

Again.

All the surgeries four years ago pour through me like a montage. So many. I felt like Humpty Dumpty back then. A very, very drugged-up egg with a shell that needed to be repaired. If he's suggesting -- implying – flat-out *saying* they're going to treat me like that again, I might as well die now.

Please let me die.

And then I see Drew's face in my mind's eye, his expression hard and determined. He's got a will of steel and he's giving me his will to get through this.

Lending it to me.

Inhaling carefully, managing my breathing, I get my throat spasm under control. I do not throw up.

"Good girl. See? You can take orders. Last time, you were just a boring old limp noodle with holes. This time is going to be so much better," Stellan says, running his index finger along my jaw. He must have a ragged fingernail, because the deep, abiding feeling of my skin being scratched, that searing hot feeling that comes from broken skin, pierces his movement.

I don't move. Then I let myself blink. Drawing on every lesson in my stupid meditation classes at the Island, I make myself remove my tongue from the roof of my mouth, imagine my organs gone to liquid, drop my shoulders, remove tension. None of this changes my circumstances, but it gives me something to *do*.

Stellan pours water in an arc over my head, blinding me, some of it in my mouth before I can regroup. Hacking as the water trickles down my windpipe, I blink and sputter, catching his disgusted look.

"Here. Drink. We can't have you dehydrated." His hand passes over my cleavage, the tops of my breasts overflowing without a bra in this tight, scalloped-neck top. "You spilled some," he says with a sneer.

"Why are you doing this to me?" Shit. I broke my first rule. Stay small. Boring. Gray rock. Don't draw attention.

"Aren't you the little prima donna! You think this is about *you*? It's all about your dad, Lindsay. You're just caught in the middle."

I go numb and ice cold. "My dad?"

"You're just a useful device." His eyes widen as he eats up my breasts with his gaze.

"Device for what?"

"To ruin the great Senator Harwell Bosworth."

"Shut up, John," Stellan mutters, giving him a glare and a head shake. "Don't tell her anything."

I force myself not to turn and follow the sound of his voice. He's behind me, John looking over my shoulder.

"It's not like she'll spill her guts to anyone." His eyes turn darker and his nostrils flare. "Except for us."

Before I have a chance to wonder whether he means

that literally, there's a knock at the door.

John and Stellan freeze.

"You call someone?" John hisses at Stellan.

Stellan comes over to me and puts the sole of his shoe on my neck. "Say a word, and you'll become tile grout."

I don't point out that we're on carpet.

Stellan's body twists as he whispers to John, "No. No idea who that is."

"Hellllooooooooooo?" says a sickly sweet, high-pitched beach bunny's voice from the other side of some door. "Hello? I can hear you in there, Drew! It's Tiffany! I need to tell you something, sweetie."

My heart sinks.

Drew? Sweetie?

I breathe in deeply again, the scent of the room making me reel. I get a hint of Drew's aftershave. His scent.

Are we in *Drew's* apartment?

Why would Drew let them bring me here?

What would Drew – oh, my God.

Is this one big set-up? Have I been played by Drew all along? Was he part of this from the very beginning and I was too naive to get that?

Panic rises up in my blood, rushing through my veins and arteries. No. No. This is what they want me to think. Drew must have no idea they're here. I stop myself from touching my hand where he inserted the microchip. These bastards are observant. Everything I do is being watched. Can't let on.

Drew will find me. He can track me, for God's sake.

John snickers and gives me a fake pitying look. "Awww. Poor Lindsay. Looks like Drew was fucking someone." He looks at his phone, which seems to have streaming video on it. A tall blonde is outside a front door. I assume this is surveillance video of "Tiffany."

I roll my eyes.

"Nice. Pretend it doesn't bother you that he's been dipping it in that dried-up old thing. Wonder how long he's been banging her? Four years, maybe?"

"What's wrong, John?" I can't help it. I say something. "Jealous?"

Stellan grabs me by the ankles and whips me out of the living room, down the hall, and rotates, shoving me backwards by the ankles under the bed. I can feel my joints snap and pop in protest, my muscles screaming, my back covered with rug rash.

"You'll pay for that," he rasps, lips an inch from my nose, his hot, nasty garlic breath making me sick again.

I let out a long moan, the sound a gasp at the end. It sounds erotic, even to my own ears.

John's nasty laugh comes from behind me. "Look at that, Stel. She likes it rough."

"Huh." Stellan releases me. "Yeah. Never would have thought."

"She wasn't exactly awake last time. Remember how you had to have us hold her legs while you -- "

Bzzzz.

John shuts up, thank God, as he answers his phone. I hear Stellan panting a few feet away. Everything in the room smells like Drew. It's screwing with my senses, with my mind as it sorts through the truth. If I lose it, I'm dead.

If I lose faith in Drew, they win.

DREW

"You can't even be outside the gates, Drew." Silas meets me about a quarter mile from The Grove. He's been expecting me. Of course he has.

"Where's Paulson?"

"Sir – Drew? What?"

"Where's Mark? He got me out of jail and I need his help."

"He isn't here."

"Where the fuck is he?"

"He's in D.C. figuring out how to spring you. Haven't heard from him for a while."

"Well, it worked. Now I need to talk to him or

Harry."

"There is no way you're getting access to the senator."

"Watch me."

"I'll shoot you on sight if I have to, Drew." Silas' voice has an icy edge.

I know he means it.

Trust me. I trained him.

I *know*.

"They kidnapped Lindsay."

"Right." Agony vibrates in his words. "We're all doing our best -- "

"Not enough."

"What's enough?"

"I don't know who to trust."

"You can trust me. And Paulson."

I shoot him a look.

"You're not exactly high on the list of trustworthy people from where I stand, Drew. Someone has to break here, and I can't."

"I need a laptop. A computer with a powerful processor."

He walks to his car and I follow. In the backseat, a black leather computer bag has what I need. A few keystrokes and he gives me the laptop. I find my way to an encrypted site and search my wallet.

"Got a micro USB adapter?" I ask him. Silas produces one almost instantly from a small ring of keys in his pocket.

I find the tiny chip in my wallet, insert it in the flash drive, and load up.

A map of North America appears and then it zooms in to California.

"Coordinates are loading," I mutter to myself.

"You're tracking her? In real time?"

"I wish. We're not quite there, but damn close. Any time she gets in range of an RFID scanner..."

The screen's processing. *Churn churn churn*. I slump against the seat and breathe. Silas reaches in the backseat and pulls out a water bottle.

"Drink this." He searches the glove compartment and hands me a small first aid kit. "There's a protein bar in there and some alcohol wipes for your cuts."

"Cuts?"

"Whoever detained you did some serious damage, Drew. You should go to a -- "

I give him a *C'mon* look.

"Right." Going to a hospital right now is the best way to get captured. I don't exist, remember?

And I need to not exist so I can make sure Lindsay *does* exist.

The screen zooms all the way in and I see a very familiar-looking aerial view.

"That can't be right. Software malfunctioned," I say under my breath. The coordinates don't add up.

"Need help?" Silas asks.

"No," I reply, terse and confused. Frankly, I do need help, because my right eye's so swollen I can barely see. The water hurts my mouth more than it helps. I pry my lips open and force myself to drink. It's better than being dehydrated. Every bone in my joints grinds with effort.

I tighten my hands into fists, pumping my blood.

I read off a list of coordinates.

Those aren't...wait.

I stare at the numbers. Pull up a new window. Type them in.

The picture the web browser shows is the front gate of an apartment complex.

My apartment complex.

"What the fuck," I mutter, sure I did something wrong. This is human error. Has to be. There is no way those bastards kidnapped Lindsay from her parents' estate and took her to *my* place.

When something makes no sense, backtrack. Double check. Verify.

I do.

Same result.

"What the hell are they doing with her in *my*

apartment?" I say loudly.

Too loudly.

"What's going on?" Silas is outside the open window, eyes sharp.

"I found her. Maybe."

"Maybe? There's no maybe with a tracking chip, Drew. You mean you found where they *had* her?"

I squint. Not hard when you only have one functional eye, but it hurts. "Looks like the chip passed my complex's RFID scanner about two hours ago."

"She's at your apartment complex?" he asks, confused. Then he whips around on me, hand moving to his weapon. "Why?" Silas' entire demeanor changes.

"How the hell do I know? They're not at the Island. Is that where Paulson is? Did he take off to try to rescue her while I was still detained?"

"Don't know."

"Silas."

"I seriously do not know, Drew."

"I need to get to Lindsay before they move her."

"Why did they bring her to your apartment in the first place?"

"Why do you think?" The realization crawls over my body.

He reels. "They're setting you up for her murder."

31

CHAPTER FOUR

LINDSAY

I become intimately acquainted with the fibers on the bedspread in Drew's bedroom. When you're stuck face down, bound by the wrists behind your back while wearing skin-tight clothes, you find ways to calm down.

Not that any of those ways work.

It's hopeless to try to manage my racing brain. Resilience is a useful trait when there's hope.

It's horrifying when any chance of escape is gone.

The mind can calculate, bargain, analyze and shift, taking in new information and discarding old as it figures out how to get back to an even-keeled state. The body, too. My muscles find micro-changes to help lessen the pain, spasms leading to more deep breathing than you'd find in a yoga class or at a pot rally.

But you can't escape your own mind. The anticipation of what these bastards plan for me makes the mind-body connection that much tighter. It's my body they plan to use for whatever sick means to an end.

All my mind can do is *imagine*.

How could Daddy have been so stupid? The soft fibers of this pale blue bedspread feel hot against my cheek as I rotate my head and try to think. Any topic other than the screaming fear that they'll hurt me is better. I replay the day's events so far. Daddy telling me about going back to the Island. My argument with him. How he said it was just for an evaluation, a few days, a break.

I knew he was full of shit. I pleaded. He said my relationship with Drew wasn't healthy for either of us. All the while, I defended Drew.

Maybe that was my mistake. Maybe I should have kept my mouth shut.

Then Mom came in the room with Anya behind her. It all went downhill from there.

My calf seizes in a cramp. As I move to make the throbbing pain stop, I widen my legs. Cold air rushes in. I'm not wearing panties.

My day has really, really gone downhill.

Like lava from Vesuvius.

Anya had seemed pale and grim, more closed off than usual. She gets that way sometimes when Mom yells at her, or when a vote doesn't go Daddy's way.

But this was different, I realize. Maybe she was pissed at me for going to Jane's house.

Or maybe she lied to Daddy and handed me off to my rapists from four years ago.

You know. A little thing like that.

If I breathe evenly, counting in fours and eights, I can fade out a little. Nothing I do will make me calm. Nothing. But I can control my breath.

Can't control my bladder, though. It's screaming for attention. I have two choices. Call for help, or pee myself.

"Oh, look. Isn't she cute. Wiggle wiggle." Stellan's voice is followed by my ass being slapped, hard. The sting of his palm sends fear coursing through my blood like a spike, an infusion of uncontrollable tension.

"I need to pee," I tell him.

He sighs, like this is the biggest imposition ever. Then I'm hauled to my feet. One ankle rolls and I'm half suspended. His fingers dig into my elbow as I squeal. He rights me, my body pressed against him.

Stellan's a well-known actor now, the kind you see on television in romantic comedies. I've heard he's quickly become the golden boy, making nearly a million dollars an episode. Fast rise upward.

A little *too* quickly.

He brings me to the bathroom. Thank God he gives me privacy, even if he leaves the door open a crack. My hands are still bound behind me. I grab toilet paper before I sit down, then realize it's useless.

"Um, I need my hands," I call out.

Heavy sigh. Stellan appears, his expression grim. "Turn around. You don't need this," he says in a chiding tone, as if it's my fault I'm wearing a zip tie.

I bite back the urge to say *I don't need any of this.*

But he frees my hands. My shoulders ache. I take one step forward. My mind has to be still. Smooth and placid like the surface of a lake. All I can do now is take one movement at a time.

And hope Drew gets here.

I sit on the toilet and can't pee. My body won't let me. A memory from an online psychology class pierces through the chaos in my emotional tornado. When in fight, flight or freeze mode, the muscles tighten.

That must include the bladder.

"Come on," Stellan calls out. "We don't have all day."

What's the rush? I want to ask him. *In a hurry to hurt me? Kill me?*

The thought doesn't help.

Think about Drew, I tell myself. Remember his arms, how he smells. Look around the bathroom. There's a can of shaving cream. A bar of used soap. A toothbrush holder with a crooked toothbrush hanging from it. The sink is messy, with small speckles on it. An electric razor is next to the shaving cream.

Huh. Wonder why he shaves both ways.

As I breathe my way to a relaxed state, I let myself indulge in imagining what it would have been like to become domestic with Drew. To come here and hang out. Spend the night. Slowly work our way toward a long-term relationship. Mom and Daddy would never put up with my living with him, but eventually we'd get married.

My ring finger on my left hand tingles at the thought. Married.

Mrs. Andrew Foster.

Years ago, I had these fantasies. I lived a life before

the attacks where I could be like any other woman, dreaming about the future. We even talked, tentatively, about what life would be like after Drew graduated from West Point.

We were just about there.

And then it was all taken from us.

My body finally releases out of desperation, the relief making me tremble. This must be what happens, I muse as I finish up and wash my hands, all my muscles trembling, legs and arms shaking. This is how we handle the imminent threat of death.

I stare at the faucet and turn on the cold water again. I cup my hands and bring water to my mouth, wincing as scrapes on my face touch the cold liquid. Drew doesn't have a cup in his bathroom.

Men are so weird.

I drink until my stomach hurts. Who knows when they'll let me have water? Out of habit, I grab the soap and wash my hands again.

Why am I washing my hands if they're about to kill me? I wonder, hysteria rising inside. Am I worried about germs?

We're conditioned by life to think in terms of cause and effect. Action and consequence. As I dry my hands, I see the raw marks from the zip tie. My Band-Aid rubbed off. I spot the pinprick from the microchip Drew put in me.

Please, I pray. *Please, God. Please.*

I stall, buying as much time as I can in the bathroom.

And then Stellan comes for me, all dead eyes and eager hands.

DREW

"Jane," I say to Silas. "Jane reported me. Mark said she reported my break-in to the police."

At the mention of her name, he averts his eyes. "Yeah. We don't know what that's about."

"I wondered. I've wondered if she was Lindsay's

informant at the Island."

"We investigated that, Drew. Came up empty."

"Doesn't mean it wasn't her."

"You think she turned against you? You think she's part of all this?" He's incredulous. I'm pretty sick of people using a tone of disbelief when they talk to me. "She was the one who found Lindsay four years ago."

"Yeah." I give him a hard stare. "How about that?"

He shakes his head, his huffing laugh dissolving into a low, gritty voice. "That's pretty hard to swallow."

"But not out of the realm of possibility."

"Everything's possible when you think the world is one big conspiracy theory, Drew."

"I have every right to wear a tinfoil hat right now, Silas."

"What about Anya? Harry said she's the one who told him that was Mark Paulson on the helicopter. Is she in custody? Being interrogated?"

His nostrils flare. "She lawyered up."

"What?"

"She's refusing to say a word without her lawyer."

"Damn."

"Doesn't mean anything. You know how politicians are. Everyone lawyers up."

"She sent Lindsay on a helicopter with the very same men who attacked her four years ago, pretending that it was Mark Paulson on that chopper, and you're making excuses for her? Are you out of your fucking mind, Silas?"

"Just stating facts."

"Facts suck."

"Welcome to reality, Drew."

"Oh, I've had more than my fair share of reality, Silas. Fuck off with the sarcasm."

"The reality is," he says, ignoring that, "Anya is tight as a drum. Senator Bosworth is freaking out, and everyone's mobilized to find Lindsay." He looks at the laptop. "We should get as much manpower on this as possible."

I ignore that.

"I can't believe Anya threw Lindsay under a bus. She had to know that what she did meant sending her to her death." My stomach roils at the thought. A vision of Anya fills my mind's eye. Cool, calm, implacable.

And *that* evil?

"She's been part of Harry's team for too long to turn on the family." I fight my internal denial. I need to be clear headed and impartial. The only bias I allow myself is toward Lindsay.

"It's hard to believe," Silas says in agreement.

This is a distraction. I need to focus on action.

"We need to regroup."

Silas says, "Jane and Anya aside, the question is this: how do we get into your apartment and rescue Lindsay?"

"*We?*" If my face didn't hurt so much, my eyebrows would shoot up. "You realize this is career suicide if you help me."

"Tell me something I don't already know."

Have I mentioned what a good man he is?

"What about Paulson?" I ask.

"What about him?"

"Where is he?"

Silas checks his phone. Taps a few times. Looks at me. "Still don't know."

"Fuck. If Jane's in on it, and Paulson's in on it, who else?"

"Throw in the senator while you're at it, Drew. How about Lindsay's mom? And me. We're all part of it. Need a little extra foil for that hat you're wearing?" He gives me a *WTF?* look. "Paulson isn't in on this."

"How do you know for sure?"

"How do you know I'm not in on it?"

"I don't," I hiss.

Neither of us breathe. One, two, three, five seconds go by.

Finally he shakes his head and slowly lets out his breath through his nose. "Then you have two choices. Let Lindsay die because you can't figure out who to ask for help, or ask the wrong person and she dies, too."

"Those are terrible choices."

"Yeah. So pick the one that gives her a chance."

I hate being wrong.

"We have to get her out of my apartment."

"You go anywhere near it, they'll know. Whatever surveillance you've got going on, theirs is better."

"Tell me something I don't already know," I reply, mocking his own words. As I speak, I crack open a cut on my lip, blood tainting my words.

"The more time we waste talking the harder this mission becomes," he points out.

"Then shut up and move."

"Move where? How the hell can we get you within yards of your apartment? They'll see us coming a mile away."

I spin through all the conceivable ways I can attack my own place. Beach? Bribe the security guard? Can't do rooftop. Can't dig a tunnel and get in.

And then it hits me.

I give Silas a hopeful look. "I have an idea."

"It better be good."

"It is. It involves gold bikinis and margaritas."

"Even better."

CHAPTER FIVE

LINDSAY

They have to feed me.

Right?

Unless they plan to kill me in the next couple of hours.

If they're not feeding me, is that a sign? Or are they just assholes who don't care about feeding me? My stomach gurgles. Then it makes an epic sound, like wet boulders being dragged through mud with air pockets.

Muffled voices provide a strange background sound. None of their words is distinct, but the accumulation of them stacks up to create a ribbon of sound. Whatever they're planning for me, they're not tipping their hands.

I'm left without a voice, without a way to get out, and without Drew.

Time keeps changing. I'm on the bed again, but sitting up against the headboard, my hands in front of me in a zip tie. It's better than having them behind me. Hurts less.

That's how I measure time now. Through pain. Less pain = easier to pass time.

Time slows when the pain increases.

I can't think forward, either. If I anticipate time, think about the future, the pain increases, too.

Mental pain.

Mental pain that will soon convert to physical pain.

What are they going to do to me?

As I move, my hair tickles my neck. Because I'm living with my skin on fire, every nerve quick and ready to react, even a gentle touch like strands of hair against my skin feels horrible. My mind keeps playing through memories of the video I've seen of what they did to me.

My gut tightens. I'm close to throwing up.

If they're going to torture me and kill me, I wish they'd just do it.

But then again, if I draw this out long enough, Drew may have enough time to find me and save me.

Which path do I choose? If I open my mouth and provoke them, I can get out of this no-man's-land. I'm stuck waiting for them to act.

I'm at their mercy on multiple levels.

You get to a point after a while when any outcome is better than no outcome at all. Where any choice is better than not choosing.

Where inaction turns you insane.

And being stuck in your own head, a prisoner to your scrabbling mind, can be worse than death.

There is a book on Drew's nightstand, crooked and jutting out. It's on top of a stack of books. I twist just enough, scooching over, moving slowly. I'm bored out of my mind and anything – anything – is better than staring at the ceiling and envisioning my own death.

My fingers gain purchase on the book and it drops onto the bedspread.

The title:

Jane's Military Aircraft Recognition Guide

You have got to be kidding me.

A laugh bubbles up, coming out like a snort, a choked gasp, the sound of disbelief and betrayal and the surreal in one bundle of air. I didn't expect *Eat Pray Love*, but are you kidding me?

My very last book I ever read will be *this*.

I'm pretty damn sure my friend Jane isn't the one who wrote it.

Jane.

Where's Jane now?

And then I wonder: seriously, Drew? This is your bedtime reading?

I have so much to learn about him.

A pang of sadness, of regret, powers through me at that thought.

I'll never get that chance. Ever. I'll never learn about his domestic habits. Does he snore? What does he wear to bed at night? Does he like the room warm, or does he open the window? Is he a spooner? What's his favorite breakfast?

What's it like to just spend time together living? Boring old daily life sounds like heaven – literally, heaven – to me right now.

I glance at the damn book. There's an airplane on the cover.

If you told me I'd stay alive, I'd read that book cover to cover every day.

My stomach growls again, the gurgle painful. I look at the bedside clock.

Seven minutes have passed since I last looked.

My eyes drift to a tiny, fuzzy gray thing behind the clock. It looks like a piece of velvet, stretched tight. It's the color of my old cat, the color of ashes mixed well from a wood stove. The gray is buried in wires from the clock. Whatever it is, I can't reach it.

Someone in the other room shouts. All the blood drains out of my hands. My heart speeds up like a scared horse.

They're going to kill me with fear. Not their hands, or other body parts, or weapons.

Good old-fashioned *fear*.

What are they doing? How can I leave a clue for Drew? I start to move toward his nightstand. Hopefully he has a pen and something I can write on. My breath draws in and out, like the wind on dry corn husks. I curl the back of my tongue so it doesn't sound so loud.

As if on cue, Stellan walks in, that creepy half grin propping up one side of his face. He's movie-star famous, but I can't see it. When someone abuses you, all objective thought disappears. No matter how attractive he is, he'll always trigger disgust in me.

But I have to pretend.

"Hey beautiful, look at you. Studying hard?" He looks at the book with genuine curiosity. Mocking laughter fills the room. "He reads this shit for fun? What a boring ass. All that work trying to outsmart us, and he thinks reading books like this will help?" He looks at me, his smile fading. "He won't be reading anything for much longer. Just the walls of a prison cell after what we do to you."

"What?" I shouldn't react. I can't help it. What is he talking about? Why would Drew be in prison?

"Don't you get it, Lindsay? Why do you think we're here? In Drew's apartment?"

"Drew would never join with you assholes. Never," I counter. Some part of me just decided. Made a split-second decision.

Apparently I have more fight left in me than I realized.

"You think he's part of us? No. Hell, no," he says with a soft, creepy laugh. "He's too soft. To easy."

Soft and *easy* are the last words I'd use to describe Drew. Ever.

"We're setting him up."

"For stalking?"

"You really are stupid, aren't you? No, not for stalking."

"Then for wh -- "

Oh.

I get it.

Oh, God.

"For your murder, Lindsay. Poor paranoid stalker Drew went over the top and killed you." He smirks. "At least, that's what the headline will say tomorrow."

I let out a laugh, a sound like tinsel being dragged through teeth. "You're planning to kill me and leave my body here, to make it look like Drew killed me in his apartment?" I go cold. So cold. My shoulders and gut tighten and I start to shake involuntarily.

But I laugh.

"We fought about it," Stellan says easily, like we're talking about a policy debate, or which Georgetown Thai restaurant is best. "I thought we should set up a murder-suicide, but we have other reasons for keeping Drew alive."

Keeping Drew alive.

"But not me?"

He gives me a sad smile. "Sorry."

He's not sorry.

Not one bit.

"Before you kill me, just tell me why." Saying the words *kill me* makes me shake harder. I blink over and over, trying to let the truth of what's happening sink in. I am alive now.

I won't be soon.

My psyche isn't equipped to think this way. Four years ago, I didn't see it coming. They drugged me, slipping something in my drink. What happened in the past happened while I was unconscious.

This? I know everything as it unfolds. This is so much worse. I didn't know it could be *worse*.

"Why? Because you deserve an answer?" he says in a mocking tone. "This isn't a stupid police procedural show. We don't owe you a monologue."

He's using acting jargon. I flatter him.

"You would know. You've been in enough thrillers. I heard about the one where you play the detective who solves everything."

"You've barely been home from your nuthouse. How would you know?"

"My mom was bragging about what a good actor you are, and how you've risen so high," I lie.

"Your mom?"

I nod and give a cynical grin, trying to match him. "Yeah."

John walks in and frowns at Stellan. "You're not here to chit chat."

"Yes, I am," Stellan argues. "Lindsay was just telling me how Monica *loves* my acting skills."

"High praise. She's a fucking phony," John says, as if they talk about my mom like this all the time.

"She's well preserved, though. Not MILF territory, but close." Stellan gives me a look when he says MILF. It's a look that makes the air freeze in my lungs.

Buy time, I tell myself. *Drew's coming.*

"Any sign of him?" John asks.

Stellan reaches in his back pocket for his phone, reads something on the screen, and says, "Jane says he's out."

Jane?

My friend Jane?

I don't say a word, but Stellan gives me a withering look. "Lindsay's piecing it together. You can see the gears turning behind her dull little eyes." He reaches for me, one fingertip grazing my body from chin to the space between my breasts. My chest and throat heave.

As his finger drops, he asks John, "He thinks it's Paulson who got him released from detention?"

"Yeah. We're keeping Paulson busy in D.C. Broken planes and bureaucratic crap. By the time Drew realizes what's happened, it'll be too late all around."

Jane. Her name rings through my head like a gong. Jane found me four years ago, bleeding and beaten and --

My friend Jane is part of this?

She can't be. She *can't*.

Because I'm pretty sure she was my darknet informant. Right before Drew showed up at her apartment, we had a conversation that seemed like she was so close to admitting it. So close, but she was edgy. Those strange looks she gave me when we met for coffee my first day home flip through my mind.

"That's right, Lindsay. Jane's in on it. Everyone you know is. You really don't understand how wide and how deep this goes."

Stellan gives John a wicked look, then they both turn to me.

"Oh," John says slowly, "you're about to find out how deep."

The world goes dark as I faint.

DREW

Finding Tiffany's phone number is easy when you have security clearance and every personal database at your disposal. Too bad my clearance has been canceled and I have to use Silas' logins for everything.

It's even easier because when I type her name into Google, turns out she has a website. But that number requires a credit card and costs $4.99 per minute, so I call her private cell.

And hope she doesn't tip off the assholes in my apartment.

"Hey," says a soft, breathy feminine voice.

"Tiffany?"

"Who's this?"

"Drew."

Silence.

"Drew from next door. The personal trainer who lives next to you."

"Oh, *sexy* Drew!" Her voice drops to a purr. "Is that gorgeous friend of yours coming over again? Mark?"

I have the phone on speaker. Silas gives me a raised-eyebrow look and mouths, *Mark?*

I close my eyes and shake my head.

He crosses his arms over his chest and stares intently at the phone.

"No, Tiffany. I'm calling about something even better."

She lets out a low whistle of appreciation. "Better than a threesome with Mark? Do tell."

If Silas's eyes get any wider they'll be planets.

"You do camera work, you said. Does that mean acting?"

"Sure! Sure it can," she says, a weird affect in her tone. I am pretty sure "camera work" means porn, but at this point, I don't care. I just need to be able to manipulate her into helping me.

47

"Interested in being part of a reality television show?"

Silas gives me a skeptical look. I explained the plan to him earlier, but he's not sold. He doesn't think anyone is gullible enough to fall for this.

"SQUEEEEE!" My eardrum shatters as Tiffany squeals. "Oh, my God, Drew! Yes!" She rushes through a series of pants and moans. "I have to call my agent! He'll be thrilled. My big break! I knew this shit work I've been doing would come to an end soon. How much does it pay? When do we start?"

"Can you start right now?"

Silence.

"Now?" Her voice is girly. "*Right* now?"

"Right now. I can be there in five minutes."

"You want to start shooting *now*?"

Yes. But not the way she thinks.

"Sure. But Tiffany, this is a complicated show. I really need your help. Don't say a word to anyone."

"Not even my agent?"

"Not until tomorrow. No."

"Okay," she says slowly. "What's this reality show about, anyway?"

"It's about people who spy on their neighbors."

"Ooooo!"

Silas rolls his eyes again.

"So we'll be filming constantly," I explain, ignoring him. "Starting now. And you'll help smuggle me into your apartment."

"Smuggle?"

"Yeah, like someone who spies would do it."

"Oh, right. We need to make this look very professional."

"Exactly. I knew you were the perfect woman for this," I answer, shining her on.

She makes an airy sound of glee.

"So what do I do?"

"A guy in a repair van is going to drive down the road in a minute. As soon as you see the van, open your garage. He'll drive in, and you'll shut the garage."

She's silent for a few beats. "That's it?"

"To start."

"I have dialogue, right? This isn't some cheesy walk-on extra part."

"Oh, no," I reply. "You're the lead actress."

"The lead?" she gasps. "This is too good to be true!"

"Tell me about it," Silas mutters.

"What do I do again?"

"You open the garage door when you see the van. We pull in. Close the garage door." I grit my teeth. Hopefully I haven't overestimated her ability to retain basic instructions.

"And cameras will be rolling?"

"Yes."

"How much?"

"How much what?"

"How much does this pay? Union scale?"

"Sure. Yes. Right."

"Okay, Drew!" Her voice is a little loud.

"One more thing – my name is Pete."

"Pete?"

"Yeah. For the show. You know. Acting."

Pete? Silas mouths.

"Can I use my regular name? Like on other reality television shows? I need the recognition. Why don't you use Drew?"

"I'm incognito."

"I thought you said you were Pete?"

I don't even bother to look at Silas' reaction.

"Watch out the window for a van. And whatever you do, don't say my real name."

"Okay." She pauses. "So that means..."

"Don't call me Drew."

"Right. You're Pete!"

"Yes." I feel like I should give her a trophy for remembering. Lindsay's life rests in this woman's hands?

"And when you're in my apartment, I should assume the cameras are on?'

"Yes. See you shortly." I hang up.

"You're crazy," Silas says.

"Heard from Mark?"

"No."

"Then this is our best option."

"You're relying on a porn star to help smuggle you into her apartment so you can covertly break into your own apartment and capture Lindsay."

"You got a better plan?"

He just inhales slowly.

"I thought so. This is the best plan. Mark got me out. He did the important part. I wish I knew where he was and could talk to him. I can't. So we proceed."

"Which means I need to get my hands on a surveillance van that looks like a handyman vehicle."

"Right."

"Be back in twenty."

"Make it fast."

He doesn't even answer as he peels out, leaving me restless.

But with a plan.

CHAPTER SIX

I hate fainting. Actually, the fainting part isn't so bad. It's the waking up that sucks. You never know exactly where you are or when it is. Your stomach goes sour and your skin shakes.

Or maybe that's just me having a terror response to waking up naked, on my back on Drew's bed, my wrists cuffed in front of me.

John and Stellan are at the foot of the bed. Electric terror pours through me at the sight.

John's on the phone. "She's supposed to deliver the information. No line is secure, so we're using mules."

Voices have an extra layer of vibration you don't notice until you're completely naked in the same room with someone who is talking. All of the tiny hairs that dot my skin go on high alert, the flesh rippling like parachute cloth being snapped on the wind. Every breath I take makes blood flow to my extremities, reminding me how much pain I'm in. My right butt cheek spasms. My knee aches. My thighs are tight with the anticipation of invasion.

Air brushes against my mons, my belly caving in, fear making me tense. They didn't split my legs open, thank God.

I have a modicum of modesty left.

It's fleeting, I know.

"Mules take too long. We've dragged this one out long enough. Time to do this right," Stellan snaps at John, who holds up one finger, as if Stellan's supposed to pause.

All the blood in my body shimmers in place, trying to figure out where to go. My breathing feels like a waterfall sounds as Stellan looks at me with cold eyes.

He doesn't see me. Lindsay. His old high school friend.

He sees a fleshbag. A tool. A pawn in a game. My survival relies on remembering that. No plea for mercy will make a difference.

John gets off the phone, then pulls a SIM card out of it. He puts it in his mouth and bites. The sound is like dry bones cracking between the teeth of a troll.

Stellan doesn't even blink at the weirdness of a guy eating electronics. I avert my eyes but wonder what the hell that's all about.

Then John reaches into the front pocket of his jeans and pulls out another phone and SIM card, inserting it in. He walks across the room and throws the old phone away.

I watch this from a detached place, like I'm at the movies and it's all intrigue.

Except this is very real.

In this film, I bleed.

"Time to do it," Stellan declares.

My stomach climbs into my throat, my pulse turning into everything.

"But she's naked."

"You're very observant."

"We were told to leave her half clothed. Staged. Remember?"

The fact that they're talking about operational details for my actual death makes a part of my mind explode.

DREW! The rest of my mind screams, joined in perfect harmony with my heart. *WHERE THE HELL ARE YOU?*

"Who cares what we were told?" Stellan walks across the base of the bed with an aggressive series of steps, getting in John's face. Tension and anger vibrate off him.

John gapes at Stellan. "We're following orders to the letter. I am done with this shit. No more having it all dangled over our heads."

"Hey, man. The price of fame."

"I wish I'd never let you talk me into this shit."

So who was the brains of it all? And fame – all three of them have become stratospherically famous in their own fields. Blaine's running for Daddy's old House seat. John's one of the top baseball players in the world. Stellan is a huge television star with a big movie career ahead of him.

The odds that all three could be so successful so quickly are impossible.

Impossible unless you realize someone very powerful has been helping them all along.

And in exchange for what?

For ruining me.

"Before you do it," I say through a numb mouth, numb face, numb heart, "tell me why."

"Why should we?" Stellan's eyes are so cold, so dead. "You won't live to process it. Analyze it. Understand it."

"Humor me?"

He laughs through his nose. "This is a waste of time."

"It really isn't." I force my shoulders to slump forward, giving him the body language I'm pretty sure he wants. Defeat etches itself in my body, and I fight to make sure it doesn't seep into my mind. I have to separate what I know on the inside from what I exhibit on the outside.

"Who cares? Just tell her. Bet she already knows. It's not like it's a secret Corning hates her father's guts." John gives Stellan a look of challenge.

I just blink. I live in two worlds right now, two sharp divisions in my consciousness. There's the part that plays along, dragging out time, trying to get information to help me understand and to give Drew enough time to find me.

The other part is having freakout emotional reactions to what I'm learning. One thousand terrified mouths are open and crying out inside the cage of my bones.

Both are important.

But only one will save me.

"Corning?" I lift the corner of my mouth. "Nolan Corning? In the senate? Daddy hates him right back."

This look comes across John's face, an eagerness and interest that would normally make me cringe. I don't, though, because I've hooked him.

And then I realize I still have some power.

"What do you want to know," I say in a neutral voice. I can hear the shake come out in my vocal cords, though. "I can tell you anything you want. I can give you information you can use."

Stellan's eyes narrow. He grabs John by the shirt and yanks him away from me. The two argue in whispers and seconds tick by.

My life is lived second by second. The chorus of terrified sopranos inside me just keeps singing. If I can make it through the obstacle course of my chaotic mind long enough, Drew will put an end to this.

I just hope he arrives before they put an end to *me*.

"She can't know anything significant. They kept her an institution all these years.," Stellan says in a loud voice.

"But she might know something about Bosworth we can feed to him."

Him. Corning. Daddy's rival for the presidency is behind this? I've met Nolan Corning a few times over the years, always at large public appearances for Congress. He's a big man with a bald head and sharp predator's eyes, jowls hanging and saggy skin making him look older than he is. Side by side, he and my dad look like Mutt and Jeff, tall and short, even though they're only five or six years apart.

Nolan Corning obstructed a bunch of bills Daddy tried to get through on transportation and energy, even though they're in the same party. He also is one of those old men who insists on kissing you on the mouth when you're a kid, even if you don't want to.

But that's literally all I know about him.

Why would he want me to be raped and tortured – and now killed? What did *I* ever do to Nolan Corning?

DREW

Cramming myself into the hidden compartment of a surveillance van after having the shit kicked out of my by law enforcement is about as much fun as you'd expect.

I think I lost half a testicle and all vestiges of self respect as Silas drives me into Tiffany's open garage. He kills the engine, the doors close, and I unpretzel myself, ignoring the pain, trying to will my half-broken right shoulder to cooperate. Adrenaline shoots through me like fireworks in the sky on the fourth of July.

It has to be enough. *I* have to be enough.

I have to get next door and save her.

What they're doing is obvious. Set me up as a crazy ex-boyfriend stalker, then kill her in my apartment. Stage the murder. Make me the scapegoat. Leave Harry and Monica in the impossible position of having hired the very man who "killed" their daughter.

It's a brilliant set up.

And I'd admire it more if I weren't the *setee*.

"Get out of here," I tell Silas as he grabs my gear. "If they start sniffing around, I'll need you on the outside."

"You can't be in here alone."

"I have to. You need to be ready with a team if it gets bad enough. Right now, we can't storm my apartment. They'll just kill her."

"Then we need to communicate on a secured line."

"Is any line secured with these guys?" Silas asks. "You're the cybersecurity expert."

"I'm not an expert. I'm just smarter than anyone else on our team. We need to up our game and find someone better than me."

"We aren't rolling in time here, Drew."

I take a few precious seconds and ponder. Closing my eyes, I clear my mind.

Time to decide.

Time to act on the decision.

"Use a secured line. This is all about to go down within thirty minutes. By the time they realize I'm there they'll be dead."

His look makes it clear he's not sure *who* will be

dead in thirty minutes, but he believes that someone will.

"I'll continue tracking down Paulson." Silas's eyes meet mine. "I want to believe he's not involved, but the longer he goes without being reached..."

"One of three scenarios is possible with Mark: he's on the other side, he's detained, or he's been harmed. Only one of those actually matters operationally."

Silas doesn't even flinch.

More proof I've trained him well.

"Let's hope it's the middle one," he mumbles.

"Hope isn't a strategy."

"No, it isn't, but there's nothing wrong with keeping some."

"Only if it doesn't get in the way of the mission, Gentian."

"Dr – I mean, Pete!" Tiffany appears, her voice dropping from a high-pitched affect to a whisper. She is done to the nines, with eyelashes that look like dead spiders attached to her eyelids.

She is wearing short shorts that make Daisy Duke look like a nun. A tight flannel shirt with breasts spilling out everywhere.

And a pink tool belt.

"Oh, my God, Drew! What happened to you?" Genuine concern floods her expression, making her look younger and older at the same time. Her hands fly to her mouth, perfectly manicured, with nail polish the color of sand. "You look awful! Did you get into an accident?"

One simple rule I've learned in my line of work: people will give you your excuse. Just pause and don't say a word. Ninety percent of the time, they hand it to you.

"Yeah," I say, grimacing."Bad bike accident."

"You ride a motorcycle?"

"No. Bicycle."

Her face falls, as if that's disappointing. "Oh. I'm so sorry."

"It's fine. Just a flesh wound, right?" I need to speed this up.

She frowns, but drops the topic. "I'm so glad you're

here, *Pete*. Who's your friend?" She goes from friendly to seductive.

"Ah, this is Joey." Joey is the name of Silas' cat.

"Joey. Love it." Tiffany shakes his hand. "You here for the filming?" She cranes her neck around him. "Where's the camera crew?"

"They're coming separately."

"Pete is here to block the scene," Silas adds.

"And you're here to..."

"Leave. Joey was just leaving. He'll be back with the crew later. I need access to the wall between our apartments, Tiffany, to do some drilling."

"Drilling?" Her eyes fly wide with fright. "I don't own this place. You never said anything about drilling!"

"All expenses will be covered by the production company," I say. It's a lie. I will definitely pay for any damage, though.

If I live.

Her body relaxes with relief. "Oh. Sure. Right. Like Extreme Home Makeover, huh?"

"Exactly," Silas says nodding as he gives me a sardonic look.

"Okay. As long as you have insurance or something in the contract so I don't get sued." Her lips pout and her eyebrows go down. "You do have a contract, right?"

"I have to go drop by legal and get them to give me the newest version," Silas says casually, like it's no big deal. Like he's not lying.

"Perfect." She looks around nervously. Her hair, long and flowing over her shoulders, moves like one piece, like a LEGO toy hair helmet. "We're not filming now, are we?" she whispers.

"No. Camera's not on yet," I says smoothly, walking past her.

Limping past her. Falling down those concrete stairs at the jail didn't do me any favors.

Lasering in on the next few action items in my sequence of events, I march into her apartment, the layout a mirror image of my own. There's a guest bathroom I'm going for. I press my ear against the wall.

Nothing.

I go into the guest bedroom.

Nothing.

Kitchen, living room – nothing.

Master bedroom – jackpot.

Men's voices, muffled and indistinct. They're in the bedroom.

Is Lindsay?

And then the voices change, coming closer.

Followed by the higher-pitched tone of a woman talking.

Emotion floods me, shoving all the adrenaline out through my pores, my body turning into air and dust. She's alive.

Alive.

Relief fills me like a balm, a cure, an antidote.

I give myself exactly five seconds to feel it all.

And then I stuff it right back in my internal box of emotion.

Feelings cannot be in charge of me right now.

Lindsay will die if I let that happen.

I pull out my toolkit and get started. Step one is simple: establish visuals.

"What am I supposed to do, Drew?" Tiffany's hovering over me, nervous. "Do I have lines? Is this improv?" She says the word *improv* like she's worshipping something.

"Yes. One hundred percent improv," I assure her. That's probably the only non-lie that I've told her. "Your first job is to go to my apartment and slip this note under the door. If someone answers the door, you're in character."

"In character?"

"You can't tell them I'm here, or that this is a reality television show."

"Won't they notice the cameras?"

"The cameras will all be hidden." I realize I need to be more persuasive with her. "You do understand, don't you?" I take on an authoritarian tone. "I need to make sure we have a professional on this show. You really are in the business, right?" I up my skepticism level to an almost comic level, hating that I have to do this. One ear is perked, listening for Lindsay's voice. So far, everything's gone quiet on the other side.

"Of course!" Tiffany gushes. "I'm a pro! I practically live on camera 24/7." She plucks the piece of paper from my hand and shuffles off, reading as she walks. "Wait. This is a note telling them I'm having work done on my pipes."

"Yes. Just a friendly note from one neighbor to another."

"But everyone who lives in this complex knows that I would never leave a note, silly. That's so rude. I would knock on the door and -- "

"No!" Panic gets the better of me for a split second, enough to yell loud so that she jumps. "You need to stick to the script."

"I thought there was no script."

"We don't have lines, but we have guidelines," I emphasize. *Get a fucking grip*, I tell myself.

And then I hear the men on the other side of the wall talking. A pause.

Followed by the sweet sound of Lindsay's voice.

"Okay," Tiffany says, wary. The way she's looking at me makes it clear she's not sure what to think, but she's going along with it anyhow.

"Just slip it under the door. If someone answers -- "

"Why would someone in your apartment answer?"

I wink. I lie. "It's part of the show."

"Gotcha. So they're actors?" She fluffs her hair, which mostly means she pushes the helmet of hair up an inch.

"No. They're unsuspecting real life people who don't know what's going on over here." Another truth.

"Oh!" Her eyes brighten. "I love being in on the joke and they don't know!"

Joke.

Right.

I look at the wall and contemplate my first move. Goal number one is to get a fiberoptic camera through a light socket or a tiny hole in the wall, to establish a visual without breaking the line. I can't think too many steps ahead, because I have to pivot if this goes south. All I can do is focus on this step.

The drill and other tools will make noise. My premise is weak. But having Tiffany go to my apartment is part of the ruse. I wait until she comes back.

It gives me a chance to assess myself. I look down. I am fucked.

CHAPTER SEVEN

LINDSAY

"What do you want to know?" I offer.

"Why would you give us confidential information like this?" Stellan asks, turning to John. "I smell a set up."

I laugh. "You seriously think I'm offering fake information? Okay. Fine. Go ahead. Go ahead and kill me. Then you'll never know if I could have told you something you could use to protect yourselves." I shrug, as much as you can shrug with your hands tied together. "Kill me. Ruin the chance." The words come out with a strange detachment as I stop caring.

I just...stop.

A switch flips in my head. It's a relief. I am my blood. I am my heartbeat. I am each breath.

But my mind doesn't matter any longer.

No one is coming to save me.

Not Daddy.

Certainly not Mom.

And obviously not Drew.

We fool ourselves every day into thinking that we have forever. Maybe we have to. If we thought about the fact that we're going to die someday, maybe we couldn't really live. Waking up, brushing our teeth, slogging down coffee, and doing whatever we need to do to check off our To Do list requires a belief that there's no end.

Because if you knew there was an end, wouldn't you live differently?

See, I know there's an end.

It's staring right at me.

"Where's the weakness in your father's security?" John asks.

Stellan smacks his arm. "She doesn't know the answer to that."

Because I don't care, I say, "Helicopter mechanic. All it takes is planting a guy on that team to sabotage Daddy's helicopter."

They stare at me.

"No way. That's what Anya said, too," Stellan whispers.

Anya. Anya and Jane. Of course. Of course they betrayed me. Betrayed Daddy. I'm beyond caring, right? The information flows over me like a river of logic. Makes sense.

But how are they connected to Nolan Corning?

Tap tap tap.

Someone's knocking on the front door.

John's body lunges, flying over me, arms and legs extended like he's a flying squirrel. I rotate slightly just before he lands on me.

Big mistake.

His hip bone digs into mine like two foreheads cracking, my left leg going up as he rolls, the pain of his jeans button scraping along my inner thigh. My hands are in front of me and some muscle in my shoulder pulls so hard the pain blinds me, leaving me screaming without sound.

I'm close to fainting again.

"Jesus, Lindsay. Be more careful." John's mocking words heat up my ear, his breath smelling like garlic and darkness. I close my eyes, the brush of my bare calf against his jeans like singeing my skin with a hot branding iron. My breasts feel heavy against my chest. The cool air makes my nipples tighten reflexively.

Shame ripples through me as they pucker. The last time that happened, the muscles moved from arousal.

Not terror.

"Get in here," I hear Stellan say to someone. The door slams shut. I can look through the open bedroom door and see sections of the hallway. Pale shadows cover the wall. A woman comes into the room, her head turned around as she still talks to Stellan, who is handling her roughly.

She turns around.

It's Jane.

Jane.

I open my mouth to say her name but nothing comes out, because John casually presses his forearm against my throat. Something pops in my neck, right where a man's Adam's apple would be. It feels like a chicken bone caught in my trachea.

I can't breathe. He's pressing so hard I can't breathe.

Her eyes catch mine. She's an animal, feral and caught in a trap, her breathing erratic, her face pale with shock.

Jane is no accomplice.

She's a victim.

I can't think. My vision swims. Instinct makes me grab John's arm, fighting. I need to breathe, my chest spasming. I kick hard, finding leverage, losing it as he effortlessly presses the palm of his other hand on my pubic bone, hard.

I'm trapped.

I'm dying.

I'm fading out.

"Lindsay! God, no," I hear Jane say as if she's underwater, except I'm the one who's drowning.

So this is how I die.

Naked in Drew's bed with Jane watching.

Where are you, Drew?

I love you.

And then the world folds up neatly into a pinpoint of light that closes in on itself to become nothing.

Just like me.

DREW

Another female voice, screaming Lindsay's name.

Fuck.

"I slid the note under the door," Tiffany says, walking on those tiny stilettos, holding a compact mirror and some kind of pale beige makeup stick thing. "But your camera crew's still not here."

"They're on their way," I say tersely. The drill has to be turned on. No time for delays. Whoever is screaming Lindsay's name is crying out for a reason.

Time is of the essence.

The drill sounds like a thousand rocks being ground up by giants using a mortal and pestle, but I use it anyway, scoring a three foot by three foot chunk of wallboard, popping it out, finding insulation. With my bare hands, I pull it out, locating the electrical outlet. My fingers feel like sausages. I'm sweating like a pig, but my throat is dry. The second knuckle of my right index finger won't move properly.

I force it to move.

"Did you just kill her?" I hear distinctly, a woman's panicked voice loud and clear. Now that the thin wallboard, exposed along with pipes, electrical wires and ducts, is all that separates me from Linday, I have a better sense of what's going on.

And this does not sound good.

"Let go of her. Jesus," says a man. Gagging sounds, then the distinct choking of someone vomiting.

"Lindsay, I'm so sorry, oh my God are you breathing? Are you okay?" The woman's voice is familiar, but I don't have time to figure this out. I slip the fiberoptic camera through the holes in the electrical outlet. It's like putting a cooked noodle through a keyhole

I attach it to the phone Silas gave me, press a button, and --

Holy fucking shit.

Lindsay's naked, on her belly, the soles of her feet facing me. She's the source of that choking sound, dry heaving, her shoulders rising up, hair spilling away from me.

The mystery woman is Jane.

Stellan's to the left and John is on the bed with Lindsay, not touching her. With a firm grip on Jane's arm, Stellan looks like he's calling the shots.

"She could give us good info, you idiot. Don't choke her yet."

Yet.

He grabs a piece of paper out of Jane's hand. "What the hell is this? A message from Corning? What the fuck is he up to, John?"

Corning.

I go cold. Sucks to be right. Nolan Corning, Harry's chief rival in his own political party, is behind everything. Processing the implications of this is impossible in real time. Absorbing the shock is critical though. This explains it all, right down to my being set up and the technology advantage – among others – that Stellan, Blaine and John have had all along.

I also realize that if Stellan is openly talking about the guy in front of Jane and Lindsay, he's planning to kill them both.

Thinking about Nolan Corning is a luxury I can't afford now. John shouts, "How the hell should I know? What's it say?"

"Says the neighbor's having remodeling work done on her apartment and she apologizes for any noise."

Bzzzzz.

I take that as my cue to turn on the drill and finish scoring the square I'll punch out shortly. The element of surprise is my only weapon.

Emphasis on *only*.

My attention has to stay on the drill, but I'm not stupid, I look at the phone screen as well. John's grabbing Lindsay and rolling her on her back. She's groaning. Jane is in Stellan's grasp, shaking. Her knees look like they're about to give out.

"Fucking neighbor getting home improvements," Stellan mutters, crumpling the note and throwing it right at the outlet where I'm observing. It pings, then bounces, rolling under my bed.

My bed.

Fury takes over, my emotions unrestrained as I watch *my* woman on *my* bed, naked and in peril. This is the first time she's ever been to my apartment, and those fuckers do it like this?

She's groaning, which means she's alive. A nasty red line crosses her neck. I see bruises and small spots of blood on her legs.

They've hurt her.

Just how badly have they hurt her?

I should have a strategy here, some sort of plan for what to do after I rescue her. Right now, the plan is:

1. Break into the bedroom and use the element of surprise as a tactic.
2. Kill John and Stellan.
3. Get Jane and Lindsay to safety.
4. Hand off Jane.
5. Run far, far away with Lindsay and tell the world to fuck off.

But numbers one and two are paramount. The rest can't happen if I don't do them.

"Look," I hear Lindsay say in a weird, strained voice. "Let Jane go. Why is she here? Just -- " Her shaky sigh makes rage run through my bloodstream. "Just leave her alone. She didn't do anything."

"Nothing other than feed you information for years when you were on the Island," Stellan says.

The room goes stone cold quiet.

I pause. Drilling sounds should be intermittent to keep up the ruse, I remind myself. But I pause to watch my phone screen.

Jane is staring at Lindsay.

Whose eyes are closed, body trembling violently.

If I'm lucky, I've got two to three minutes left to get in there and save her. The clock races faster than my pulse. I have to catch up.

The toolkit contains the simple tools I need to

penetrate the wall, but it also has a sniper rifle in there. I need a clear line and a few seconds to pick off one of them.

The problem is what will the second guy do?

"I don't know what you're talking about," Jane and Lindsay say in unison. I ignore them, turning the drill on again, scoring the wall. I penetrate slowly, feeling my way so I go through the wallboard just enough to be able to kick out the chunk I score, but not enough to pop through the other side. That would make what I'm doing obvious.

And that could kill Lindsay.

"Shut the dumb bitch up," Stellan says, followed by a weird ripping sound. Muffled, higher-pitched sounds come through the wallboard, but I keep a steady hand as I cut the wall. Then I look at my phone.

They've taped Jane's mouth shut.

And John is ripping more duct tape for a go at Lindsay's face.

Once you mute a person, you remove a distinct part of their humanity. If they won't let Lindsay talk, then they're done with her. If they were smart, they'd pump her for information, but they're not smart. They're tools of evil and evil, apparently, doesn't give a shit what Lindsay knows.

She's a tool, too.

One that gets the job done by being dead.

I finish scoring the square and grab my weapon. Then I pause, closing my eyes, imagining in my mind's eye the next set of steps. Muscle memory can't be accessed for this set of maneuvers. I have to go deeper, to the part of me that runs entirely on instinct, with a singular goal:

Save Lindsay.

Everyone else is collateral.

Including me.

CHAPTER EIGHT

LINDSAY

I can't breathe.

Duct tape covers my mouth, my tongue retreating as the cold, sticky tape smacks over my lips. If I were thinking, I'd make sure my tongue protruded so I could fight the tape later.

But I don't believe in "later" anymore.

Later is a luxury for people who have a future.

I sink into the bed, my body a tense noodle. I've collapsed and given up, but my muscles haven't received the message yet, tight and reactive, ready to flee or fight.

I can't do either of those, and I already froze.

Time to just wait to be killed.

"Let's do her first," Stellan says to John, looking overtly at Jane.

Stellan walks quickly, a flash of movement out of the corner of my eye, and suddenly my face is on fire.

The shock of having the duct tape ripped off my face makes my jaw pop, my mouth screaming in agony, tears filling my eyes and making it impossible to see.

"Before we do that, I want some answers from Lindsay after all," he says, giving John a series of weird looks, his eyes flitting to the wall to my right.

What the hell is so interesting about that wall? Someone's doing maintenance work next door. Who cares?

"Leave Jane alone," I choke out, looking at her. She's gagging, and I hope she doesn't throw up, because she'll suffocate to death. Tears stream down her eyes and she's just standing there, completely shut down, John holding her arm, giving Stellan hell.

"Fuck off," he says to Stellan. "You keep changing orders, and we're running out of time,"

"Why are you doing this at all?" I croak out. "You won't tell me why me, but tell me *why*. Why do you want to do this?"

Stellan lets go of Jane, who crumples to the floor, as if she's been held up entirely by his grip. He moves with catlike grace, a sickening athleticism to his motion. It's captivateing.

I'm captivated.

Or just captive.

His hand reaches out, my body jerking in strange movements as I struggle to breathe properly, my throat still swollen and hot from John's choke hold. The sizzle of his skin against mine makes my abdominal muscles curl in, as if they're trying to roll me away from him. Protect me. Secure me.

"Oh, Lindsay," Stellan says in a sad voice, as if I've disappointed him. He sounds like every teacher who realized I didn't understand a math concept, like my mother after a campaign appearance where I didn't smile enough, like Daddy when I tried to do better.

"You really are naive, aren't you?" With an attitude so close to tenderness it re-ignites my fear sensors, he reaches into his back pocket and pulls out a blade.

Jane's on the floor, scrambling to stand up, breathing hard, making little mewling noises as she spots the knife.

Instead of cutting me, my braced body flinches as I hear the snap of the plastic zip tie around my wrists being cut. Then he holds the blade up to my face, poking lightly at the soft, thin skin under my right eye. One tiny move and he'll pierce my eyeball. I can't blink. Can't flinch. Can't react, because I could be the instrument of my own blinding.

Carefully, almost theatrically, Stellan lowers the knife, folds it in half, and shoves it in his back pocket. His hands cup my face, cradling my jaw as he studies me, tilting his head to and fro, eyes crawling over my features like he's determining my value.

Like an appraiser at an antique show.

Like a courier delivering a sex slave.

And then he kisses me. The gesture throws me into a strange place inside, like I'm at a freak show carnival and I'm one of the acts. Everything goes crooked and off key. My lips are cold, still stinging from John ripping off the duct tape, and feel like soft plastic. Stellan's lips are warm and wet, slippery with power as he pulls me roughly to him, my nipples brushing against the fabric of his button-down shirt. With Drew, this would be erotic, arousing, pleasurable – maddeningly ecstatic.

It feels like death with Stellan, as if I'm a corpse and he's kissing me, my blood stopped and my heart a cold piece of meat in my chest, unyielding.

I cannot react. I hold my breath, hoping he'll stop, knowing he won't.

Then he pulls away and gives me a loving smile that doesn't match the violent look in his eyes.

And he slaps me so hard across the face that I fall off the bed into a heap, at Jane's feet.

"Because," he says calmly as Jane sobs, bending over to help me, my hair covering my chest, my nakedness on display, "because we *can*, Lindsay. If you could do anything you wanted and know you'd never be caught, what would you do? How far would you go?"

"This – this isn't some stupid horror movie, Stellan!" Jane blurts out as her hands slip under my armpits, gently helping to prop me against the wall. He must be wearing a ring, because there's a nasty slash on my upper eyelid, a long, hot cut that feels like lightning.

"Oh, God, shut her up, too," Stellan says. "She's just an extra."

John grabs Jane, who tries to struggle, but she keeps looking at me. She knows I'm her fate. Whatever they do to me, she's next.

"WHY?" I scream. "Why? Just because you want to isn't a good enough reason. It's weak. You're weak. You're just doing this because someone's pulling your strings. You're too stupid to pull this off on your own." I harden my voice, taunting them on purpose. Why not? What the hell do I have to lose?

Stellan's taste is still in my mouth. I breathe slowly, imagining his cells floating out of me on my outbreath, evicting him from my body.

"You think we're the stupid ones?" John barks, laughing. A drill next door starts up again, the sound louder, closer. John and Stellan move even closer to that wall, giving each other those disquieting looks again. Whatever they're planning to do to me, it's imminent. Any second now, I won't be alive.

DREW! my mind screams. I can't stop thinking about him, how he's failed me, how all my hopes and dreams are gone now.

My last gasp of hope fades out as I stand, shoulders back, and walk across the room, confronting them. If I'm going to die, I'll do it on my terms.

I won't be a scared little rabbit anymore. Not for these last seconds of my life.

John's eyes narrow, and Stellan flattens his palm against the wall, annoyed by my presence, his other hand moving in an arc, ready to hit me.

So I grab John by the back of the neck and make him kiss me.

DREW

Is she *kissing* John?

Is Lindsay really kissing John *by choice*?

Completely shocked by what I'm seeing on my screen, I hesitate, then regroup.

My mission hasn't changed.

I'm still here to save her.

But is she kissing him because this is all part of some sick plan of hers?

Or worse – is she in on her own kidnapping?

I reel back. The world ripples, like I'm underwater

looking up through crystal clear blue water and a rainstorm begins.

Then it clears.

The reason she's kissing him like that has nothing to do with saving her. Divorce the thought, Foster.

Analysis later.

Action *now*.

"The pipes look good," I call back toward the hallway in a disguised voice, Tiffany rushing over, looking worried.

"Okay, Pete!" she says in an exaggerated voice as I flip my phone screen over. The last thing she needs to see is a naked woman in a bedroom with another woman and two guys next door.

Then she whispers, "Where's the camera crew? I've got everything ready."

Everything is ready? I don't know what she means by that. I don't care.

"Good," I say loudly, dropping my voice.

"Is your nice friend coming back? He said he'd get the camera equipment and be back soon, to start filming." Tiffany frowns. "I want to make sure I'm doing everything I can so this is successful. I need to move up the ladder in my career. I hate what I do for a living now." She shrugs. "It pays the bills, but..."

Her nattering becomes background static as I think about what's happening on the other side of this thin wall. Lindsay's kissing John, walking naked around that room – my bedroom – like she owns the place.

"Drew – er, Pete?" Tiffany's long fingernails are digging into my bicep. "You listening?"

"Sure." No, I'm not. I'm calculating and trying to figure out whether Lindsay is so smart that she's able to override every fear response in her and act in a self-preserving way that is highly risky, or she's played me all along.

And you known the damnedest part?

Either way, I still love her.

"So that's okay?' Tiffany interrupts, looking at me

like she thinks I've been listening to her.

"Sure."

She gives me a kiss on the cheek and scampers off.

And then my fucking phone rings.

I leap up, whack my head on a towel rack, and my phone goes flying, cracking on the tile floor with a sickening sound of a screen shattering. My tools go everywhere, and Tiffany squeals.

The phone still works, thank God. I don't recognize the number, but that's not new. I ignore it.

I flip back over to the scene in the bedroom.

Lindsay and John are kissing like they're in the backseat of Daddy's fancy car on Prom night.

Stellan's leering at Jane.

My stomach falls through the floor, blood picking up speed like it's a horse in the Kentucky Derby on its last leg.

What the fuck am I supposed to believe right now?

My phone rings again. Same number. I pick up. maybe it's Silas on a new line.

"Drew? Jesus, Drew, get the fuck out of there." It's Mark Paulson.

"Mark? What? Did Silas tell you -- "

"I'm not the one who got you released from jail, Drew."

"What?"

"I didn't get you released. I was in D.C. with my Galt, trying to use every connection we have between the two of us. I was obstructed and stalled in every way you can imagine. My dad said he'd never seen anything like it, and if Galt Halloway can't get shit done, you know there's something deep at play."

"You're saying Stellan, Blaine and John got me sprung?"

"I'm saying," Mark says slowly, as I watch Blaine Fucking Maisri waltz into *my* bedroom and rip Lindsay and John apart, then turn and say something to Jane, "that you've been set up even more than you ever imagined. Whoever got you out of jail, and whoever blocked my dad and me from getting you out, has power that goes all the way to the fucking top."

"Where are you, Paulson? And why should I trust you? You're telling me you're not the one who got me out, and -- "

"Drew, you don't have a choice. We're on our way."

Can't trust Lindsay, can't trust anyone. I look at my screen and there's Blaine, on top of Lindsay on the bed, and she's screaming.

I feel the screaming in my bones.

And then the screaming ends, abruptly, like a snapped wishbone, like a twig turned to kindling, like death is a fulcrum you use to break everything to pieces.

"No time. They're going in for the kill now, Mark. Now," I whisper, hanging up.

And then I ready my weapon as Blaine cups Lindsay's breast, his hand going lower, lower...

My leg's ready to kick in the panel. Milliseconds before I deploy the kick, John leans down, his face filling my phone.

As I let all the kinetic energy in my body release, my gun in my hand, my mind a blank slate, he says, "Hi, Drew."

CHAPTER NINE

My hearing's shut down, the sound of my own blood rushing through me so strong, I almost miss the splintering gasp of wallboard breaking. Drew crashes into the room like something out of an action movie. He's holding a weapon in each hand and Blaine's on me, his cock rubbing hard against my thigh through his pants, his wet mouth demanding my lips, my tongue, my attention.

A sound like thunder in my ear makes me scream, biting hard on Blaine's tongue. I taste copper and pain, then he twitches and trembles, the violent shakes so bad I feel electrocuted.

And then he slumps forward, deadweight, crushing me.

Can't breathe.

Can't hear.

Can't see.

Can't *anything.*

Oh, thank God.

It's over and I'll just faint and fade out and be nothing and oh drew oh drew i love you and please please please --

Someone shoves Blaine off me and my world is bright and big and full of pain.

Loud crashes, my throat being squeezed, and eyes that fill with love and horror aimed at me.

For me.

It's Drew.

I'm covered in blood, all over my belly and thighs. I

look like I got my period but it's too far north, congealed in my navel, stroked along my lower ribs like warpaint, like feathers dragged through holiday paint.

I'm bleeding.

But I don't feel like I'm bleeding.

John and Stellan are screaming. John has a gun at Drew's head, pressed right against his temple, while Stellan's holding his knife to Jane's throat.

There's a huge, human-sized hole in the wall, pipes in the way, tufts of pink insulation poking out like cotton candy, begging to be eaten.

Nothing makes sense. There are too many sounds, too many movements, so much motion and light and dark and space. The air's scent rife with blood and fear, all our musks mingling to make for sour promises and tangy loose ends. I don't move because I don't have a framework for what it means to move. I don't speak because I'm not certain what words are.

I just look at Drew.

And he stares right back, unreadable.

Has he given up, too?

No. Impossible. He can't have given up, because he wouldn't have crashed through the wall. Wouldn't have killed Blaine. Wouldn't be standing there, chin jutting up, facing off with John and Stellan.

I know backup is coming. Mark and Silas? Someone else? Drew wouldn't do this rogue.

"Hello!" A high-pitched, fake voice comes through the hole in the wall. "Is there a party in there? I just love -- "

"We'll be right there, Tiffany. Stay in your apartment. Go to the living room," Drew yells.

"Fine," she says, never coming into view, her voice full of bitter acceptance.

Stellan glances at Blaine's body. A giant dark stain is pooling under him, right where his head is. The room's turned into a dark tunnel, with two points of vision for me, so I'm not sure what I see. I reach up to rub my eyes and my hand is gooey.

Blood.

Blaine's blood.

"What a good idea," Stellan says slowly as John taps on his phone with one hand. "Let's go over to Tiffany's place." He shoves Jane through the hole in the wall before she realizes it, her head whacking the wallboard, a long, angry scratch forming on her neck. I see it in slow motion.

Time is distorted.

Drew looks at my naked body with an expression of chilly evaluation. I search his eyes, needing any form of emotion to show. A twitch, a blink, a micro-expression that tells me he cares.

He's a robot.

John and Stellan make us huddle in the other apartment's living room, where Tiffany gives me a horrified shriek and screams, "Pete! What the fuck? I'm trying to get out of porn. I don't do this torture shit!"

"Shut up!" John screams, the gun on Drew the entire time. "Say one more word, bitch, and I splatter his brains all over your couch."

"But that couch isn't paid for yet!" she wails, dissolving into a puddle on the floor.

Who is Pete? My brain isn't working with all cylinders. I look at Drew, who looks at Tiffany.

Who winks at him.

Winks.

A wave of ice-cold nausea pours over me like someone's dumped a bucket full of slush on my head. Is this a set-up? Is Drew in on this somehow? Is that why he came crashing through the wall – because he knew damn well that the guys took me to his apartment.

Because he *let* them?

How far does this game go?

All the tension in my body drains out and I sit on the couch.

"Hey! Blood!" Tiffany squeals.

I ignore her, grabbing a pillow and hugging it, wanting a tiny sliver of modesty. Of warmth.

Of something.

"This isn't a snuff film, is it?" Alarm fills Tiffany's wide eyes. "Because I didn't sign on for anything like that."

Her voice goes to a whisper as Stellan glares at her. "Shut up or I'll shut you up," he says.

She complies.

"I can't believe he fucking killed Blaine," John says to Stellan, clearly unraveling, his hair soaked with sweat, face oily, left eye twitching.

"You think he won't kill us both if he gets the chance? We can't give him that chance, John," Stellan replies, dropping the knife from Jane's throat. He shoves her toward me. She sits on the couch.

I move away.

"Lindsay, I swear I'm not in on this," she says under her breath. "They threatened me once they figured out I was your Island contact. My mom had no choice because they -- "

A loud popping sound, like a wet bag of sugar being tossed from a moving car, makes me jolt. Jane's head rockets into my lap, a big indent in her forehead directly over her right eye. I didn't know that bones could *dent*.

I reach up and touch my own eye socket, the one they reconstructed four years ago.

I guess I do know.

I didn't see my own beating, though.

As Jane moans, the vibration from her throat makes my thighs tingle. Her head is on the pillow and she's making this bizarre gagging sound. Her breathing speeds up, from zero to sixty, and then she starts to choke-scream, like she's drowning.

It's all happening in my lap and I can't do anything but stare dumbly.

And then she passes out.

One long, rattling breath comes out of her, and then she sighs, a thin, drawn-out sound that makes me think she's dead. Another breath comes, then another, and soon she's intermittently making shallow, then deep, sounds.

"Get off the couch," Stellan orders. I gently put

Jane's body on the ground at my feet, a process that takes longer than it should.

"This is really good acting," Tiffany says to Drew quietly. "Pete." Then she winks again.

What the fuck is wrong with this woman?

Drew ignores her.

I'm cold. I'm hot. I'm dry. I'm wet. My senses have wires that cross and connect, that are frayed and bent, until I'm just a series of nerves and impulses that have gone haywire. I don't have feelings like a normal person because none of this is normal.

None of this is right.

None of this is real.

Maybe if I decide this isn't really happening, I can make it go away.

I close my eyes.

And then Drew says, "Nolan Corning's already turned you in to the police. You have five minutes left before they get here. Go ahead. Kills us all. It won't matter. You're either rotting for the rest of your lives in prison, or you're dead."

DREW

Tiffany gives us all a strange look and before Stellan or John can say a word, she laughs. "Nolan Corning? He's that asshole on television going on all the time about... about..." She frowns, then waves her hand in the air. "About government stuff. I see him on cable news. Is he -- is he a guest star, Drew? I mean, Pete?" She looks around the living room, craning her neck, then grabs the remote. "See? I'll bet if I turn on the television he'll -- "

John hits her hand so hard the remote goes flying into her wall-mounted television and rocks the screen, a spiderweb of cracks marring the glossy space. Tiffany must have pushed the button just before he hit her, though, because the screen comes to life.

"Oh, my God, the production company damn well better pay for this!" she shouts, giving me a nasty look.

"What the hell is this, Drew? You never said the television show would be about guns and knives and naked women with blood. If this is some kind of joke, I -- "

Tiffany's blonde helmet moves in slow motion as Stellan takes the hand with the knife in it and goes after her, slashing down like a pro, ripping open a long line down her bicep. I take the opportunity, grabbing his wrist, feeling the web of my hand slice open as Stellan attacks. His free arm goes around my waist, feet kicking under me to try to make me drop.

I catch him off-guard as blood drips into my eyes from Tiffany's wound. She stumbles back and then I can't see, the blood blinding me.

I flip to pure instinct, eyes closed, body engaged.

He's taller, wiry, with muscles that feel smooth and big under my palm but he's buff in a practiced way. Stellan's body is designed for a specific function, not for fighting. From the ground, I kick up, making him fall and taking the single second of advantage to be on him. Something hits my shoulder, a hard, thick object.

The knife.

I feel around for it, failing, then put both hands on Stellan.

But his reflexes are fast, and he's on his feet before I can let go, dragging me forward. My chin whacks the floor, sending fireworks behind my eyes, a molar cracking in the back of my mouth.

"Get the fuck away from me, you bitch!" he shouts, then he's out of reach as I take a hand, wipe my eyes clean, open them --

And see a naked, blood-covered Lindsay holding the knife.

She dips into a squat, her right arm at an odd angle, the knife blade up but clutched hard in her filty hand. Using her thighs, she pushes her body up, turning it into a missile, the kinetic force of her full being in the strike she makes.

And she hits Stellan in the crotch, all three inches of metal blade sinking into his body.

That's not enough.

Not for her.

Like a gardener hacking away at overgrown vines, she pulls up, hard, with brute force movement designed for function. She grunts with the strain, a war cry, a battle call. There is hypnotic beauty in her motion. I watch with grotesque reverence.

Stellan's entire groin soaks burgundy, like he's spilled a glass of Pinot Noir at a dinner party, an oaf, a dork, a clumsy man who can't even handle his drink.

Reflexively, he reaches out, both hands forming a perfect circle around Lindsay's neck, her breasts bobbing as he squeezes so hard I hear something snap in her neck.

And then I burrow the knife further in with a drop kick that makes me grateful for punting practice back in high school. I hit her hand and want to pull back, but force myself to give it my all.

Stellan drops her neck and falls backwards, pushed a few feet by my blow.

Click.

I look up to find John holding two guns, one at Lindsay's head, one at mine.

"Go ahead," he says with a grin.

"Make my day," Tiffany finishes for him. Her sad eyes meet mine, her good arm shoving a pillow as hard as possible against her nasty wound. "That's the old line, right?" She starts to shake. "By the way, I don't have health insurance, so your television show better cover this."

A groan like iron plates grinding together comes from the heap of flesh called Stellan, his eyes glazing over, hands fruitlessly patting at what used to be his cock. Lindsay's turned it into ceviche.

"Corning never told us this could happen," John says through gritted teeth. "This wasn't part of the deal when we told him we'd rough Lindsay up four years ago." Safety's off on both his weapons, and he has the haunted, hunted look of a man who's coming to reckoning.

"Rough Lindsay up?" The fact that I just watched my

girlfriend turn one of the men who ruined her life into a eunuch has me firmly convinced she can be trusted. I want her to look up, to check in, to give me a chance to read her and understand her next move, but she's just a wall of tangled, dirty hair.

"Yeah. It was supposed to be in good fun. Slip her something, get on camera, make her look like a slut, ruin her dad. You know." He shrugs like he's describing how he cheated on a test.

"And me?"

"You were all Stellan's idea, man. He wanted insurance. Said you'd go nuts and ruin us."

He casts nervous glances at Stellan, who is still breathing but clearly nonverbal. I hope the motherfucker is in so much pain every single sperm is screaming.

"That's not fake blood, is it?" Tiffany says, hysterical, as she watches Stellan pass out. "Oh, my God!" Her panic winds up, her eyes catching everyone's looking around the room.

Then she looks at the television and screams,"We're on TV!"

Hysteria can do some fucked up damage to people. I ignore her.

Lindsay, though, looks up and focuses her attention on the television screen.

Then she smiles.

The look in her eyes makes me flinch, so I turn and follow her gaze.

The split screen on the cable news show displays us. Here. Right here, in Tiffany's living room.

Live.

"WHAT THE HELL IS THAT?" John screams, his voice going high.

"...new footage, a second videotape from the attack on presidential candidate Senator Harwell Bosworth's daughter, Lindsay, shows a shocking discovery: Hollywood actor Stellan Asgarth, major league baseball player John Gainsborough, and up-and-coming California state

representative Blaine Maisri all unmasked and all involved in sexually assaulting her unconscious form. Digital media experts confirm that the video footage is real and undoctored..."

The cable news announcer's voice is flat and unemotional until her voice goes into a gasp, then the live feed from Tiffany's apartment goes black for a few seconds, resuming with Lindsay's naked body pixelated to cover her nakedness.

"We've received word from some webcam fans of a woman known on the Internet only as 'Sexonda Beach' that fans witnessed the live feed in her apartment and altered law enforcement when men with guns, knives, and a naked woman suddenly appeared on camera. Police crews have been -- "

"HOLY FUCK!" John shouts.

"I knew my live feed would come in handy some day!" Tiffany gushes.

"WHAT ARE YOU TALKING ABOUT?" John screams.

And then it comes together for me. Tiffany's "camera work."

Sexcam work.

"I run a live streaming webcam show from my house," she explains, standing slowly, walking over to a fern and waving her good arm. "Before Drew came over, I made sure my live feed was set up so they could all cheer me on as I filmed my big break." She blows a kiss at the fern. "Hi, guys! I love you! Thank you for taking good care of me!"

Tiffany looks at her bloody arm, and drops like a sack of potatoes into a dead faint.

"How did they get my secret video!" John screams, his voice climbing into high registers of the doomed.

"Your video?" I ask, balancing ten thousand threats on the head of a pin as I try to get him to keep talking just long enough for me to disarm him.

Lindsay looks at Jane, then grins maniacally at John. She has blood in her teeth.

"Jane did that. Hacked your system. Funny how a 'dumb bitch' outmaneuvered you." She makes a weird, over-the-top huffing sound. "Two dumb bitches."

She looks at me. "I told you I had a plan."

My God.

She's *luminous*.

John looks around the room as sirens peal in the distance.

He's at his most dangerous now. I have to act.

He pauses. Catches my eye.

And then he pulls the trigger on the gun pointed at Lindsay.

CHAPTER TEN

I think that memory is like a mother. It protects you when you need to be sheltered from a cruel world.

It forces you to face reality head on and develop a tougher skin.

It tells you that all that really matters is being kind and good and decent.

And reminds you that you are more than the sum of all your parts.

The bullet rips into my shoulder as I drop to the ground, sensing what John's going to do before he does it, a mantra of *Fuck no you don't* whipping through my mind like blood in a centrifuge. I fall on poor Jane, who is a warm lump under me.

A body – *Drew!* -- arcs over me, just like Superman, arms outstretched, torso elongated like he's faster than a speeding bullet.

Except Drew isn't.

The bullet got me.

John falls on top of me and his hand goes to my throat, then he's off me, dangling in air like a puppet, his head snapping to the right in an unusual angle. How does he do that? It's like a special effect, only this isn't CGI and when he falls to the ground, Drew behind him, his arms pumped, his face berserk and ferocious, eyes on me.

That's where my memory steps in and says *enough*.

Wood splinters in the distance and then the room is filled with men in black and heat, an impossible number of guns, and they're all crowding around us, Silas and Mark

Paulson barking orders, Drew screaming my name as the men in black fatigues cover the room with their red lasers.

If I weren't in pain, so hot, so cold, so wet, so tired, the bouncing red dots would make me laugh.

And then I'm off Jane, on the couch, a blanket on me, someone pressing hard on my shoulder, making me scream. Drew's above me, his mouth moving but the words aren't there. Who pressed his mute button? Someone turned off all the sound in the world.

Stretchers appear in my peripheral vision and then the warm blanket is off me, cold air stinging the lava-hot part of my soul. I don't have a shoulder anymore, just a place where the heat all lives. I open my mouth to scream but I stop, bracing myself.

Then I exhale, so slowly it's like blowing through a straw.

And I don't care.

The pain doesn't matter.

Drew's staring intently into my eyes but I can't look back. It hurts. He thinks I'm here but I'm not. I left. I left back in that bedroom with my mouth on John's, his lips a sick caress of the damned.

I close my eyes.

"We're losing her!" Drew says.

Are you? You're losing me?

Good.

I don't want to be found.

DREW

I let Paulson grab my arms and pull me back only because the med crew is there to put oxygen on Lindsay, to stem the flow of blood from the gunshot wound, to save her.

"You saved her," Paulson says in a voice meant to shake me out of my reactive mode.

"She's unconscious!"

"She's in shock," he says, shifting to a calm civilian tone. "She's not going to die, Drew." He looks pointedly at Stellan's body, the section from the waistband of his jeans to mid-thigh a blanket of blood, the handle of the knife poking out from his crotch like an obscene joke. He looks like an extra from *Bad Santa*. "Unlike some people in this room, she won't die."

I follow his gaze and watch Stellan's chest.

No movement.

He's definitely dead.

Jesus. Lindsay did that. I watched her stab him. I helped by kicking the knife home. There is a reservoir of pure strength inside her. I've always known it, but to watch it in action is a form of strange beauty.

They're all dead. All three of our tormentors. A group of SWAT officers, Mark, and Silas start talking to me in serial, each question too loud, too swift, too perfectly pointed for me to focus.

The medical personnel wrap Lindsay in thick blankets and prepare to move her to a backboard. Once she's secured, they put her on a stretcher, one person applying pressure to the gunshot wound, the others pulling her away.

I gravitate toward her.

I meet a wall of men.

I go around them.

Mark's hands are on my shoulders, rock solid, unyielding. His hold communicates a distinct message.

You're not going anywhere, Drew.

A high-pitched whine fills my ears, an industrial sound like a pneumatic wheeze, the sound of machinery and motors functioning in the distance. It's louder and louder, and soon I don't understand Mark's words.

Instead of focusing on him, I watch the television, which has cut away to an aerial view of my apartment. Tiffany is next to the television, surrounded by paramedics, and she's breathing in a paper bag. The look she gives the female medic who hands her an oxygen mask should make my heart hurt.

Can't hurt something that's locked away in a box, though.

"You did it," I hear. I turn sharply, following that voice.

It's Silas.

"You did it, Drew. You said you'd get them, and you did."

"We did." I look toward the doorway where the paramedics are maneuvering the stretcher with Lindsay on it. I step forward, but Silas gently blocks me.

"You can't go with her."

"Why not?"

"She has a GSW, Drew. They'll get her to the nearest hospital then med-flight her to LAC."

"That bad?" Shock ripples through me. I'm doubly determined to follow.

"You've broken so many laws. We have to take you into custody."

"That has to wait." I push past him. He lets me, but Mark's right by Tiffany's front door. He's a wall, a barrier, a border between me and Lindsay.

"You have your own wounds, Drew."

I brush him off. "I'm fine."

"Looks like you broke something in your left hand, and you're limping. You're not fine."

"I'm fine. I'm not letting her leave without me. I'll ride in the ambulance with her."

"No."

"Fuck you."

"No to that, too. You don't understand how bad this is."

"And you don't understand how bad this is going to get if you don't let me go with her."

"Is that a threat?"

"It is what it is. Let me go with her, damn it."

"I can't. I have to take you into custody."

"What?"

"You just killed a man on live television, Drew. So did Lindsay. Jesus Christ, millions of people just watched this scene as it unfolded! You killed two people here. I can't just let you go."

"Then take me to the hospital with her." I start coughing. I taste blood. I lick my lips.

His face fills with alarm and he waves a medic over. "Pull up your shirt," Mark orders.

"What?"

Without asking, he grabs my shirt. My belly is covered in nasty bruises, bright red marks deep. I inhale sharply and feel a diffuse pain, spreading through me like sunshine when you're camping in the pines in the northern woods, that moment when the sun pours through and chases the cold away.

"You could have internal bleeding." He's somber, glaring at me like I've done something wrong.

I cough again. More blood.

"No. I have to go with her -- " The coughing fit consumes me, followed by a sudden tightness inside my gut, like someone's twisting and pulling a rope in me. My organs are playing tug of war. I'm aware of thirst, then pain, my eye fuzzy, vision weird. During the lead-up and the fight, I fought it all off.

The body remembers.

The body demands to be heard.

"God damn it," Mark snaps, holding my arm. "We need another stretcher for him!" he shouts as a strange pounding fills the room, like thousands of soldiers in formation, headed for war on a hollow gymnasium floor..

"I'm fine." Cough. "I'm -- "

I'm tired.

So tired.

And then I'm not there.

CHAPTER ELEVEN

One day later...

LINDSAY

The nurse's assistant comes in at four a.m. to take my temperature. She flips on the lights. Fluorescent lights suck. I don't say a word. She comes to me with the thermometer, sticks it under my tongue, pushes something on the handheld machine, then waits. She hums a jazz tune. I'm an obedient patient.

She records the results and leaves, turning off the lights.

I shift in the hospital bed, my mouth dry. I swallow, then gag. I need water. I look at the pitcher on the table-tray above my thighs.

Might as well be on the moon.

My one good arm has a million tubes in it, covered with so much surgical tape I look like a mummy. But if I don't drink, I'll keep gagging, and when I gag or cough, my shoulder screams out in heated pain.

So I have two choices.

Suffer or suffer *more*.

Not really a choice.

Like an inch worm, I move to my back, then feel for the bed controls, my good hand fumbling. They're tangled in the sheets, but I get them eventually. Pushing the button to raise my head is an art form, one I haven't mastered.

Because this is the first time I've done it.

I woke up around midnight, groggy and unreal, with

no one here. Someone noticed. I think I'm in ICU because of a sign I read. The doctors called my name, flashed lights in my eyes, asked me to nod and squeeze their hands. I did everything they wanted.

Except speak.

I can't.

Okay, I probably *can*. But I can't. My voice is broken. Just like my soul.

It's not raw or injured. The mechanics of verbalizing are present.

But the part of my brain that connects to my mouth to interact with other people is gone.

Poof.

I have no will to speak. I have no will to speak because that requires looking at people and being looked *at* and emotional demands and processing and I just can't.

I *won't.*

My body is naked under a thin hospital gown, covered with a sheet and few of these warm white woven blankets. I have a tube sticking between my thighs and I jolt as I move up. It's in me.

In me.

I freeze.

Then I realize it's a catheter. Gross. Screw that. I reach down under the covers and remove it, not caring, tossing the tube off the end of the bed. I can pee on my own.

I have to be allowed to control *that.*

I push the remote button to move the bed because I'm starting to die if I don't get water in my mouth.

Maybe I press the wrong button because instead of feeling the bed move, the nurse's assistant rushes into the room. She's followed by two people in scrubs, a tall man with dark brown hair and kind eyes, and a short woman my age who smells like peppermint tea.

"Hey there," says the man, who reaches for my good arm, touching the biceps with a warm palm. "Look who's getting feisty."

The short woman frowns at him and gives me an eye

roll. "That's not patronizing at all." She expects me to react. To smile. To join the joke.

I don't.

I can't.

I appreciate the attempt. They don't understand. They're trying to talk to Lindsay Bosworth. They're trying to connect with someone they assume is a whole human being with a distinct self, with plans for the future and a rich inner life. Someone who has emotions and nightmares and memories of the horror she just experienced.

But that Lindsay doesn't exist.

They're interacting with a fictional character they've created in their well-meaning minds.

"Your parents will be here in two hours. Six a.m. sharp, we told your father. He's been so worried," Dr. Brown Hair says, his eyes showing he's troubled by me.

"Your mother, too. We couldn't get her to leave yesterday," Dr. Short Woman says with a snappy tone. "She's a stubborn one." She looks to me for a reaction.

I just stare ahead, then close my eyes.

And wait for them to leave.

But no.

They're not going anywhere.

Dr. Short Woman grabs the pitcher of water, pours some into a cup, and pops a straw in. "Here," she says, tapping my good hand. I raise it and grasp the cup, slowly moving it to my mouth. Twice I miss.

Third time, bullseye.

The water is a relief. I swish it around, moistening everything, removing some of my suffering. As I swallow, they watch me. They expect me to react, to emote, to speak.

I just swallow and breathe.

I rest my head against the mattress and put the half-full cup on the stand.

"Higgs, take a look," Dr. Short Woman says to Dr. Brown Hair, who I guess is actually Dr. Higgs. She's pointing to the end of the bed. "She removed her catheter."

He frowns. "Maybe it fell out?"

"*Over* the covers?"

They look at me with a new level of interest.

Dr. Higgs smiles and shrugs. "I guess we can consider her ambulatory now. No more catheter. Lindsay can use the bathroom on her own."

"Lindsay?" Dr. Short Woman says in a worried voice. "Can you speak?"

I nod.

"Would you please speak?"

I shake my head and sigh.

Nothing they do for the next five minutes can pull me out of my shell. If I wait them out, they'll leave, and the I can just be alone with my pain.

Someone adjusts an IV. Dr. Short Woman presses a piece of plastic into my good hand. "This is for pain medicine. Push it whenever you need a dose. You can only get one dose per hour, though. It will help you sleep."

I push the button.

And wait.

By the time they leave the room, my pain is hovering in the corner, watching me like a spirit that doesn't know it's dead.

Drew

"I mean it, Harry. I'm not leaving until I can see her." I'm squared off against him, face to face, right outside Lindsay's hospital room. After a torturous night in my own hospital bed, and debriefings and interrogations from more law enforcement agencies than members of a baseball team, I'm here.

Battered, bruised, and checked out of the hospital against medical advice.

But here.

"Drew," he says, his voice compassionate. "Monica is on her way. Lindsay just woke up a few hours ago. We have her under careful guard. Let us see her first."

"Of course. But I need to see her after you."

"That might not be good for her mental health. The trauma..."

"You think I don't know about the trauma? I witnessed most of it."

He flinches. "So did half of America, on national television. That live feed complicates everything."

"You mean having your naked daughter on television cutting off her attacker's cock may hurt you in the polls."

"You think I'm that cold?"

Before I can answer him, Monica sweeps down the hall, her face lighting up as she sees me.

I experience déjà vu. Last time she looked at me like that was four years ago.

"Drew!" she gasps, pulling me in for a fake hug, two fake kisses on my cheeks. She's a cloud of perfume in female human form.

Those eyes express genuine emotion. "Thank you for what you did, Drew. You're the one who cracked this all wide open." Her side eye glare aimed at Harry leaves nothing to interpret. She's pissed at him. "Unlike some people," she elaborates, "you weren't snowed."

Harry just clenches his jaw and sighs.

"Then again," she adds, leaning in, "we could have done without the whole world seeing Lindsay naked like that. The live feed was brilliant, though."

I give Harry a look.

"We haven't been debriefed yet on all the specifics. But Nolan Corning is in custody, has already resigned from the senate, and an ad hoc investigation committee is underway. We know now that he reached out to Blaine, who pulled John and Stellan into the mix. Their goal was to paint my daughter as a whore, to discredit me, to derail my future in politics. Corning had one hell of a web he weaved to make that happen." Harry gives me a cold look I can't read. "Unfortunately, the perpetrators are all dead. We have you to thank for that."

"Only two of them. Lindsay killed Stellan all on her own."

Harry grimaces. "Right." He looks sick. "I've seen

the video. Your drop kick helped."

No reason to respond, so I don't.

Monica nudges Harry, then looks around to see if anyone's watching. "Did you thank Drew publicly?"

"Yes."

"Now we have ample proof that Lindsay was drugged. Jane found the video Blaine Maisri made of that horrible night four years ago. The scheming little asshole had it as backup, just in case someone turned on him."

A vision of Maisri on top of Lindsay as he attacked her in my bedroom makes my eyes move rapidly, my heart speeding up.

"Drew?" Monica's manicured hand covers line, the bite of her French-tipped fingernails cutting through memory. "Perhaps you need more time to rest." She gives the door to Lindsay's room a nervous glance.

"I'm fine," I insist.

"No one is fine, Drew," Harry declares, rubbing his palm across his chin. He hasn't shaved, and his tie is loose. Monica's the picture of perfection, but Harry's unraveled a little. "No one."

"Duly noted," I say, relenting. "But I'm better than Lindsay. That damn gunshot. If John had better aim -- "

"But he didn't," Monica says firmly. "He didn't, and you saved her. We have a mess to wade through, but it's a mess with a daughter who is *alive*."

"They were so close," I admit, my voice dropping as I fight the tightness in my throat. "Too damned close."

Harry's eyes go unfocused, the light shining on them. "None of that matters now. We have to deal with the situation at hand."

Something in his words makes the skin around the base of my spine tighten. "What does that mean?"

"Lindsay's up. Her reflexes are fine. She can answer yes/no questions. But she's refusing to speak."

"Did she have a brain injury?"

Harry shakes his head and blinks rapidly, shoving a hand through his hair. "No. Nothing that would explain this. According to the doctor who attended to her two hours ago, she made it clear she won't talk. Not that she can't."

"What? Why?"

"We don't know," Monica whispers. "Shock? Trauma? She was kidnapped, hurt, stripped naked..." Her voice fades out, eyes hardening. "And then paraded all over every cable news channel, covered in blood and...well, you know the rest."

I certainly do.

"The trauma from that would rattle anyone," Harry rasps. "We're hopeful she'll ease her way into talking."

That tightening in my back turns to a tingling warmth that sets of a hinky meter inside me. I think eight steps ahead, projecting what they're saying.

"I'm sure she'll recover quickly," I say, more to myself than them. "A gun shot wound is no small experience."

"You're been shot before?' Harry asks.

I shake my head. "I've been damn lucky, but I know plenty of people in the field who have been. You don't just magically heal. It's a different kind of injury. Give her time." I make eye contact with them both, pressing a point I can't say. "Lots of time."

"We'll try, but the jackals are everywhere." Harry looks pointedly down the hall, where camera crews crush the double doors leading to this ICU wing. "They've had two people slip in pretending to be medical staff already. I'm not sure how much longer we can keep her safe."

"She needs time."

"She needs privacy."

"Silas and Mark are doing a great job," I insist.

A tall doctor with brown hair, brown eyes, and the build of a hockey player appears. He has a nasty scar on one eyebrow, and he's wearing scrubs, a lab coat, and a name tag that says JONAS in big letters.

"Dr. Jonas," he says, reaching for Harry's hand, then Monica's, shaking them with great ceremony. "We'll take you in to see Lindsay now."

They go into the room. As I look around them, I see

her on the bed, her right arm immobilized, her body covered in pure white sheets and blankets. Machines beep with soothing regularity, tubes connecting from IV bags to her arm.

My phone buzzes. I damn near jump out of my own skin at the sensation, but shove my hand in my pocket and check, my broken finger forgotten momentarily. Gingerly, I use my other hand to find the phone. It's Paulson.

Be at the hospital shortly. Have new information.

Silas approaches me with a tray of coffees, motioning with his chin for me to take one. I grab a white cup and sip, not caring what I drink. It's black coffee. My tongue burns with the hot liquid, but I don't care. Sensation of any kind that distracts me from Lindsay's condition is good.

"Heard you signed yourself out of the hospital against doctor's orders," Silas says, setting the tray of coffees down, taking one for himself. Clearly, the other two are for Harry and Monica.

"You're nosy." I slug down more liquid pain.

"Just doing my job. My boss is a stickler for detail."

"Which boss? Paulson or more?"

"Both."

I raise an eyebrow and drink.

"I'm sorry we couldn't get there faster, Drew."

"You did fine."

"A few more seconds and we might have saved Lindsay from being shot."

"No. A few more seconds and John might have grabbed her and played hostage with her. Those seconds before you crashed the place were unpredictable."

"I saw the footage."

"Who in the world *hasn't* seen the footage?"

He shrugs. The entire nightmare has been played on international television for the past day. Post-mortem analysis follows the same basic news cycle script. It all becomes pretty simple once you know who was trying to destroy whom.

Nolan Corning decided four years ago, when Harry

was making his bid for a second senate term and also clearly shoring up a path toward the White House, that this would not do. For all of his political career, Harry had been a teflon man, impervious to scandal.

Corning needed a news story so big it would bury Harry forever.

How he reached out and found Blaine Maisri is anyone's guess, and I know we'll find out in the coming days and weeks. Killing all three attackers was, in retrospect, terrible for investigating what happened, but in the life-or-death heat of the moment, you don't pause to consider the future.

And Lindsay's moves against Stellan were self-defense. The video makes that clear.

Even if the knife plunge made every man who's watched it sit with his legs crossed.

Silas snaps his fingers in front of my face. "You there?"

I ignore him and drink half my coffee, staying quiet.

"That video Jane released to the media, the one with Blaine, John and Stellan not wearing masks? It's been proven to be legit. She hacked into his hard drive and got it somehow, along with some coded notes between an aide in Corning's camp. The rest will fall in place as the search of all their electronic records unfolds."

He's trying to reassure me.

I can't stop staring at Lindsay's door.

"Drew?"

"Heard you. Good. I want the least bureaucratic mess for Lindsay. Her recovery is more important than media time or interrogations."

"Investigators have to interview her eventually."

"Not without me present."

"You're still not cleared yet," says a deep voice from behind me. Paulson appears, wearing a crisp suit, a well-ironed shirt, a dark purple tie with grey accents, and a look that says he wants to kill me or give me a medal.

Could go either way.

"I don't give a shit about being cleared. I'm staying

here until she talks to me. If that were your woman in there, you'd do the same."

He nods. "I would."

"Any news?" Silas asks Mark, finishing his coffee and tossing it in the trash bin like a three-pointer. He misses, makes a face, and bends down to throw it away properly.

"Yeah," Mark says, anger evident in the way his nostrils flair, the posture he assumes. "This thing goes all the way to the top, and has tentacles everywhere. When Galt and I tried to get you released, Drew, turns out NSA, CIA and FBI operatives were all part of the effort to help set you up."

"I got the full alphabet thrown at me," I say, impressed.

"Galt figures someone finds you to be very, very dangerous," he adds, eyebrows up. "That's high praise from him."

"And you outsmarted them all," Silas intones, voice low.

"We still don't understand how the hell Corning has that kind of reach, and -- "

Just then, Monica and Harry emerge from the room, eyes hollow.

Oh, no.

Mark stops talking and gives Harry a worried look.

Monica grabs my hand, and says softly, "You can go in now. Maybe you'll have better luck than we did."

What the hell does that mean?

LINDSAY

I am turned slightly away from the door. I smell Drew's aftershave before he even sets one foot inside the room. My stomach flip-flops.

Not yet.

Not now.

I'm not really here. I don't want to be here. I don't want him to see me like this.

I don't want anyone to see me like this.

No. Scratch that.

I don't want anyone to see me *ever*.

Too much of me has been seen. Too much of me has been stripped naked before the world, bloodied and bruised, my fury worn as my only weapon and exposed for consideration and judgment. Stellan didn't just kidnap me. He stole me. He stole me and delivered me to John and Blaine and they took my humanity – again – and turned me into an animal.

Only this time, I was awake for all of it. Aware. Sentient and breathing and afraid and terrified to the point where I just can't be who I was before.

He stole who I am and scraped it clean off me, like a car stripped of all its value, the important parts gleaned, the rest an empty shell no one wants.

A nuisance.

A pile of non-functioning junk.

The sound of Drew's even breath makes me close my eyes and slow my own respiration. If I pretend to be asleep, maybe he'll go away.

His scent gets stronger. I feel heat to my right, like he's radiating it outward.

Even though my eyes are closed, I can tell when he's next to me. He doesn't touch the bed. A shadow changes the light behind my eyelids, and his heat intensifies. There's more than simple warmth there. It's a kind of compassion that takes on temperature, as if goodness can be calibrated to produce light.

I don't deserve that.

I know he's in pain. I know I should reach out, should heal, should work together with him.

If nothing else, he should be thanked.

But the thoughts tumble together with hard, sharp edges of memory. The shards of terror embed themselves in my bloodstream, floating like inner tubes on a lazy river, waiting to be caught on rocks and long, thick logs made of dead trees that just haven't rotted to pulp yet.

If memory is a mother, protecting us from the worst the world throws our way, then the present – the achingly slow *now* that rolls out second by second, never rushed by intent or desire – is a bully.

The present hurts me right now. It hurts to be here, to be aware, to be so close to Drew and yet so far away.

He has no idea how distant I really am.

And frankly, neither do I.

"Lindsay." My name coming from his mouth brings me back to his bedroom, a place of sanctuary and passion that was destroyed by Stellan, John and Blaine. When I hear his voice, all I can see is Blaine on top of me, groping, his hand a final insult as I gave up on Drew.

I say nothing. I'm dying a thousand deaths inside. I slow my breath. Maybe if I slow down enough, I'll just stop on my own, winding down like a toy that finally rests, tilted toward mother earth, inertia drawing it to a close.

"I know you're here."

No, Drew. You're wrong.

I'm not.

The pain medication button is in my hand. I press it so hard the first joint of my thumb turns cold.

"I am so sorry," he whispers. I can't look at him. If I did, I know I would see tears.

I can't look at him because that is what a whole person would do.

And I am just a shell.

"I am so proud of you," he adds. The scrape of a chair against the tile floor tells me he's here to stay. The sound is like nails on a chalkboard. I don't react.

How can I?

I'm not here.

"Please open your eyes."

I don't.

"Lindsay. I know it hurts. I know you feel like you are dying inside, like you're trapped in a big black hole with nowhere to grab. I know it. Grab onto me. I'm here. *Grab onto me*. Take whatever part of me you need and hold on to it, baby. Borrow a piece of me until you can find that part of yourself. Please. Don't do it for me. Don't do it for your parents. Do it for you." He doesn't touch me, but his hand goes on the bed, next to me. It's shaking.

His voice is trembling.

My soul is an earthquake.

My heart is a tsunami.

And like any force of nature, there's nothing anyone can do to stop this. It just is.

I fade out, the medicine doing its job, thank God. My eyelids crack open slightly. Out of the corner of my eye, I see his head bent down, broad shoulders in a suit jacket, the fabric stretched tight.

His hands are clasped on the bed next to me.

Like he's praying.

Chapter Twelve

Drew

"I brought you maple creams," I say, holding out a five pound box of chocolate-covered candy for Lindsay to ignore. For the last three days, I've visited her every day.

And for the last three days, she's refused to communicate. Eyes closed, breathing slow, body tense. She has no idea that I understand. I do. I get it more viscerally than she could possibly know.

And that's why I'm not giving up.

She can ignore me.

But I'll keep coming back until the day she doesn't.

When I woke up in my own hospital bed four years ago, sore and bruised and in denial, I let that dark slimy part of my soul take over. It's the insidious voice that tries to convince you that life is nothing but an endless, monotonous series of seconds you have to endure because you have no value. By letting yourself be victimized – yeah, I said it, *victimized* – you're forever tainted. Weak. Stupid and foolish, easily suckered.

And that will never change.

Physical pain is bad enough. Time halts in place when you experiencing it, as if being graciously polite, giving pause to recognize the searing interruption. You can't rush time. You can't get through being at the receiving end of someone else's intentional pain because you don't count.

You're not important.

You have no will.

It's not even about losing control, because everyone

loses control. All of us have moments where we are at someone else's mercy. You have two choices:

Reduce the opportunity for that to happen *or* hope that when it does happen, they aren't evil.

And if they are?

Well...I don't know.

I still don't know.

I wish I had the answers. I'm just a guy showing up day in and day out to pry his girlfriend out of the little fortress she's hiding in, hoping a five-pound box of sugar might help.

You think I have the answer?

I'm as clueless as anyone else.

And that pisses me off.

I set the open box next to her, down by her thighs. Her gunshot wound is healing enough that the dressing is smaller, less bulky, and it looks like she has more mobility. There's a deck of cards sitting in front of her on the bed tray, a rubber band around them. A cup of red juice and some of her favorite potato chips sit there, tauntingly normal.

"If you don't eat one of those, I'll have to give them to the nurses, and they'll flirt with me. Please don't make the nurses flirt with me, Lindsay. One of them looks like she's a box of chocolates away from pinching my butt."

Nothing. No response.

I know from the doctors that she communicates with nods. Makes noise when she's in pain. Harry and Monica talk about her "choice" not to talk, but I know better.

There is no choice here.

She *can't*.

If I'm right, Lindsay is on her own, an astronaut adrift in space, enough oxygen to make it through each day but with the lonely terror of the unknown gaping before her, so silent it's piercing, so darkly beautiful it hypnotizes you at the same time it paralyzes.

You just float.

But you float in a bleak abyss. It's a painful infinity, numb and cold, blinding and agonal.

And I have to break her out of that internal jail.

She's a prisoner of circumstance, locked away in her own mind. No one can pull you out of it. You have to decide for yourself.

But I won't stop offering her a hand.

I won't stop offering her a lifeline.

I won't stop, period.

I sit on the edge of the bed, the closest I've come to her since I began visiting every day. She tenses even more. Her eyes are closed. I know she's a box full of emotions. With her eyes closed, I have the luxury of studying her face, unhurried. The bruises are a motley explosion of haunting shades of blue, purple, and a yellowing edge on one, her black eye fading slightly. Tiny cuts cover her face, neck, and the skin leading to her bandaged shoulder. She's so ethereal, even with so much injury.

I want to hold her. Wrap myself around her and wait her out. I want to be the shield for her.

I got there in time. She's alive.

But was I somehow still too late?

"I love you," I say with a reverent heart, closing my own eyes, my hand inches from hers. All the movement has to come from her. I can't pull her to me. I can't push myself on her, emotionally or otherwise.

She has to reach out for me.

Any other path isn't authentic.

And doesn't help her.

After a minute, I realize my breath has changed. A new pattern has emerged. I'm breathing with her. I open my eyes to confirm it.

Our chests are in sync.

And one single tear rolls down her cheek. It makes a prism, reflecting the blues and purples and browns and yellows of her cheekbone, her jaw line, her neck as it meanders from her emotional core down to the heat of her skin, buried in the folds of her body.

And still she breathes on.

It's something.

It's hope.

I'll take it.

My damn phone buzzes. I ignore it.

I want to touch her. I want to reach for her hand. The connection is what I need. I think she needs it, too. Every night before bed my mind fills with live electricity, finally settling down abruptly, my subconscious delivering me into slumber like a light switch being flipped off.

I do not dream.

For that, I am grateful.

I will, though. Soon. I know how this goes.

The nightmares emerge when you've healed to the point where you can find a rope to pull yourself up just enough out of the abyss to begin to see a crack of light.

Paradox, right?

No one ever said reality was easy.

The short female doctor comes in, makes eye contact with me, then looks at the football field of chocolates on Lindsay's bed with a raised eyebrow.

Her eyes flit from Lindsay's face to mine. Her mouth sets with a grim determination.

"Can I have one, Lindsay?" she asks.

Lindsay nods.

I jolt.

The doctor shrugs, plucks a candy from the box, right smack in the center, and makes notes on a chart. Her throat spasms as she chews and she gives me a grateful look.

"Those are amazing."

"Her favorite. *Your* favorite," I stress, looking at Lindsay as I stand, the bed moving slightly as my weight comes off it.

No reaction.

"Can we talk for a moment in the hall?" the doctor asks.

I leave with her. She pulls me aside and whispers, "I can't give patient information, but because you have security clearance, I'll tell you this: half the nurses hate you for bringing all this candy, because Lindsay's parents send it to the nurse's lounge."

"What about the other half?"

"The what?"

"The other half of the nurses. You said half of them hate me. What about the others?"

Her eyebrow goes even higher. "They want to..." She looks away. " -- *date* you." It's clear that "date" isn't what they'd like to do.

I laugh. "What's their favorite?"

"Silas," she says, without thinking.

"Excuse me?"

"Oh!" She blushes. "You meant favorite *candy*."

My turn to arch that eyebrow.

"Anyhow, Mr. Foster," she says hurriedly. "I wanted to let you know that Lindsay does react emotionally after your visits."

I nod, looking back at her room. Lindsay's eyes are closed, her breathing even.

"Any idea when she can leave the hospital?"

"I can't share that information."

I nod. The tiny rectangular window in the metal door to her room has wire mesh between two panes of glass, criss-crossing my view of her.

Do I go back in? Do I just leave? What do I do next? How do I achieve an optimal outcome?

Through the window, I see Lindsay open her eyes and look to the left, then right.

She leans down, uses her good hand, grabs one of the chocolates --

And pops it into her mouth, chewing slowly, eyes closed. I shake my head slowly as I walk away.

Victory comes in so many forms.

LINDSAY

"Oh, my God, girl, someone loves you dearly. Are those chocolate creams?" Myles, my nighttime nurse's assistant, picks up one and sniffs it. It's eight p.m. and two different nurses have tried to get me to eat another maple cream, but I can't. Not in front of them.

They left the giant box on my bed tray, though. I've had three so far.

Fucking Drew. I don't want to like them. I don't want to want them. I don't want to have volition.

"Maple cream!" Myles squeals. He's this big Jamaican dude with the best accent and a thousand-watt smile that makes his crazy dreadlocks seem even bigger. His eyes are the color of whiskey, startlingly mellow on his face, with long lashes and a slanted look that makes him seem so chill all the time. So comfortable in his own skin.

Of all the nurse's assistants, he's the most gentle, fussing over my arm in the blood pressure cuff, or carefully moving my IV lines so the veins don't hurt.

I've haven't even been here for four days, but he's my favorite.

"You know it's my mission to make you eat one of these in front of me, right? Life's too short to be stubborn about chocolate. Who brought you these? Your parents? Do they own a candy empire?" he teases, knowing damn well who my parents are. The entire staff had to be vetted.

I just look at Myles, who grabs three creams and crams them into his mouth.

And smiles.

I know what he's trying to do. He chews and makes a note on a little electronic device, then does all the basics, checking my blood pressure, my temperature, my pulse oxygen, and he offers to walk me to the bathroom.

I shake my head.

Myles pulls a chair next to the bed and reaches for my hand. He catches my eyes. His mouth sets with determination. I'm about to get lectured.

Damn it.

"Listen, Lindsay. I know from your chart and the news and a lot of whispered rumors that what you went through was a crime against humanity. I won't rehash it, because I see your heart rate climbing already."

Instinct makes me look at my monitor. He's right.

"And it's none of my business -- "

Right again.

"But -- "

Here it comes.

"That man loves you. I happened to be working the floor when you were brought in, and one of my friends worked on your man when they brought him in. He's got a set of bruised organs like an apple got thrown in a clothes dryer." Myles makes a low whistling sound that makes my stomach clench.

"He's the kind of man who isn't going away. You understand that? Men like that don't give up. Not ever. There's something in you he loves dearly. He's not going away."

I can't look at Myles anymore, so I turn away. He drops my hand.

"Sorry if I crossed a line. but he calls the nurse's station every day, checks in with your security team, and I think that if we had a spare room on the floor he'd find a way to live here. You got yourself a good one. Know that."

I lift my hand and nudge the box of candy toward Myles without looking at him.

"You want me to to take this to the nurse's station?"

I nod.

He does, without another word.

I breathe slowly, counting to twenty, trying to wash his words out of my mind. He's right. But it doesn't matter. Drew's devotion doesn't matter. Drew's persistence doesn't matter.

None of it actually, materially matters.

Because whatever he sees in me that he loves so dearly – it's not there.

It can't be there.

If it's there, then I have to feel again.

And I'm not putting myself through that pain. I know how this works.

Once I start feeling again, I can't stop.

And that's its own form of torture.

* * *

I'm naked. Daddy's announcing his run for the presidency and the audience is filled with a thousand people who look like John, Stellan and Blaine. They're all holding red, blue and purple balloons. They're clapping. Grinning,

And chanting my name.

"Lind-say! Lind-say!" they shout, the chorus louder and louder as someone nudges me to step on stage. I'm wearing stiletto heels. My calves scream, my thighs shake, and my breasts bounce as I'm shoved, hard, toward Daddy. He's standing at a podium in the middle of the stage, klieg lights blasting from above, and he has an angry, frozen smile on his face.

"Go out there, Lindsay! You're embarrassing us!" Mom hisses. I'm on my hands and knees and can hear her from behind me. The room gets cold, a swift gust coming from the crowd. I look up, and all the faces are covered by a gray mist that swirls, turning into demon faces that fade and form, morphing as an ill wind blows.

"Go!' Mom shouts. I turn to look at her, my nude ass pointing her way, and all I see is Nolan Corning.

His face splits into an evil grin.

And then he's on top of me.

The crowd goes wild. "Lind-say! Lind-say!" they chant. They start to clap as I struggle to get away from Corning, but he's attached to me, like his skin is made of tape. He's an icicle, jamming at me from every angle, my skin pierced by his cold, cold body. My heart skips beats, my knees weaken, and I hunch over, curled into a ball, waiting for it to end.

Just make it end.

Then he snarls and all the cold turns to hot flesh and fur. I try to crawl away and a putrid scent fills my nose. I gag. I put one hand forward and move with him on top of me. The crowd goes silent and as I look out, opening my mouth to scream for help, I see the auditorium is empty.

The brutal nighttime sky is above us, clouds covering the moon like Congressional staffers burying a scandal, and I'm shivering, my body torn, my mouth bruised by some demon that kisses me until I can't breathe. My throat spasms. My lungs are seared shut.

Stellan appears, the high school version, then Blaine. He's wearing the suit he wore when we went to homecoming in high school, and he hands me a corsage, clipping the silver elastic band around my wrist.

I look down.

It's a dead rat.

I scream, but the sound just goes backwards, as if my own cry tries to escape from my toes, but can't. Oh, God, the pain the pain the endless pain. Where's Daddy? Where's Mom?

And then relief. I'm alone, in a river of blood, on a scarred wooden stage with the stars above. The cloying trickle of red helps me to stop shivering. I look over my shoulder for the source.

Stellan, John, Blaine, Tara, Mandy, Jenna and Nolan Corning are piled in a heap, eyes dead, bodies draining.

And when I look to my right, the auditorium seats are back. A single spotlight shines on me, showing my nude body, showing the flow of all my enemies' blood.

A lone person is in the audience.

Drew.

He claps silently.

And whispers --

"Lindsay!" Myles shakes me, touching my face with a wet washcloth. I'm clawing my face, and my wrist burns. Someone's pinning down my bad arm and my shoulder burns. "Lindsay, honey, it's just a dream. Just a bad dream," he soothes.

"Drew," I rasp, my voice sounding like rusty guitar strings being plucked by claws. My eyes stay closed and I breathe through my nose, the sound like a train coming over and over again through a tunnel. Myles' hands are warm and big. He's worried. I don't have to open my eyes to tell.

The fluorescent lights are on above me and as I open my eyes I squint, closing my eyes against the assault. When I open them, I see Silas in the tiny rectangular window of my hospital room, looking in.

Somber.

Worried.

Then he picks up his phone.

I know who he's calling.

And if I could speak to him, I'd ask Drew one question. *One.*

What was he about to say?

Chapter Thirteen

Drew

I'm alone in a chair, with thousands of similar chairs surrounding me, the cavernous space filled with a fine mist that tastes like oranges and pixie dust dancing on my teeth. I'm naked, then clothed, a flash of outfits passing over my body like an old-fashioned Rolodex being flipped.

Then I'm walking barefoot on sand, dodging IEDs, running with an American flag streaming behind me.

It is riddled with bullet holes. Each hole in the sacred fabric bleeds.

Suddenly, I'm in bed – my bed – my ceiling a cloud formation, stars twinkling behind the clouds, appearing here and there as a light breeze reveals them. Lindsay's hair hangs over my face, tickling my nose, and I'm deep inside her.

She smells like warm apple pie and sweet spun sugar, the tangy taste of her juices on my mouth. We kiss with a wet, lush openness that makes me crave her more. Being inside her isn't enough. Rocking her to ecstasy, her body stretching out as she tips her chin up to the stars, isn't enough.

I'll never, ever have enough of her.

For now, though, I'm in heaven.

My hands slide up her long torso, peaches and cream skin that stretches until it's marred with blood, the long lines of rib turning the color of old rust. Her ribs stand out in stark relief until my fingers strike steel.

I'm touching a xylophone.

She's turned to metal.

Our eyes meet and she's a robot, all glitter and automaton. My cock feels like an icicle, and then poof – she's gone.

And I'm back in the auditorium again, clapping alone.

I look on stage and there she is, her long hair covering her face, dripping over her bare breasts like honey. She opens her mouth and sings the most haunting melody, a siren call that hypnotizes me until I can't stop clapping, cheering, calling for her to go on and on and on.

My phone buzzes.

I pick it up and whisper, "She's back. Lindsay is back."

I wake up to the buzzing of my phone. Someone is calling me. This isn't a text. I shake off the dream and answer.

"Foster," I bark into my personal phone, then grimace. What if it's my sister, or Monica, or --

"She's talking."

It's Silas.

"She's *what*?" The smell of disinfectant assaults my senses, making it hard to listen. My apartment was scrubbed clean by professionals after being cleared as a crime scene by police. The blood stains are gone, but the room feels damp and haunted. Silas and Mark offered to met me stay with them, but I'm determined not to let the past get to me.

They do not get to ruin my future, too.

"Lindsay had a nightmare and said your name."

Five thousand electrodes charge my body and I sit up, a cold sweat suddenly exposed to air as my sheets roll off me. "She said my name?"

"That's what the nurse's assistant said. Lindsay spoke the word 'Drew' clearly."

I'm breathing heavily, still half in dreamland, processing Silas' words. "I'll be there soon."

"No rush. She fell back asleep. But Harry and Monica have an eight a.m. meeting with the doctors and Harry wants you there."

"Me?"

"Yeah. I was as surprised as you sound."

"Gentian?" I go back to calling him by his last name. "You sound jaded. You're too young and green to be jaded."

"Jade *is* green, sir."

If only he could see my eye roll. I grab clean underwear and head to my bathroom, my shoulder groaning in protest, my broken finger taped and throbbing. I stay on the phone as I strip down and turn on the shower.

"It's four a.m., sir. No need to shower and come to the hospital this early."

"Can't sleep. I was planning to get ready and do some work."

Hitting someone produces paperwork.

Killing people produces mountains of it.

"Need help?"

"No. Thanks, but...stay on duty. Watch her. Make sure she's safe. I know we're pretty sure we got everyone involved. Corning's in custody, we have access to John, Blaine and Stellan's electronic records, and Anya and Jane are being investigated. Still..."

"I know. It's always the adversary you didn't think about who gets you in the end."

I chuckle at hearing my own words parroted back to me.

We end the call and I step into the steamy shower, avoiding the mirror and careful with my broken finger. All I'll see is a bruised torso, cuts everywhere, and a fading black eye. The medical staff at the hospital considered me "lucky" after I described my sequence of injuries. I've been through worse.

This is like running a 5K vs. a full marathon on the spectrum of injuries.

Hot needles of shower spray wake me up, washing the dream off me. What did it mean? Was it a premonition, given Gentian's call? I don't believe in metaphysical bullshit. Give me facts.

Evidence.

Conclusive proof.

But the dream, the call, this feeling I can't shake all add up to something.

I have no idea what.

In a few hours, I'll find out.

* * *

I hate conference tables.

I hate conference tables in hospitals even more.

After my parents died in a car accident while I was in Afghanistan, my sister took care of all of the basics. I flew home for the funeral, but we spent one horrible afternoon in a hospital – not this one, thank God – discussing body transport to the crematorium, final billing issues for the medical care my parents did receive, and a host of bureaucratic details that turned the shock into something halfway comforting, a strange morphing that only rigid systems can achieve.

Processes and routines matter when your world has been blown to smithereens.

And while Lindsay hasn't died, I have a similar feeling right now as Harry and Monica file into this tiny room, followed by Dr. Higgs and the short female physician I now know is Dr. Belzan. Lindsay's been in the hospital now for eight days.

Eight.

And every one of those days, I've come here and tried. Silas told me the nightmares started for her a few nights ago. He told me the smile on my face was creepy. I tried to explain it away. I gave up.

She still won't talk to me. Won't talk to anyone.

That's okay.

She will.

"We've invited Drew to sit in for this briefing," Harry explains. Silas is outside, on duty still. He refuses to leave until this meeting is over, then he's coming back to my place to hang out. His directive, not mine. I shift in my seat, my ribs aching. The internal damage that was done to my spleen looks like it's healing. I won't need surgery.

"We're at a crossroads," Dr. Higgs explains, a folder in front of him. "Lindsay's medical progress is solid. The gunshot wound tore through the typical tissue and tendons, but she was lucky. It didn't hit bone, just soft tissue. She should be ready to be discharged in a couple of days."

"We can take her home?" Monica asks, smiling. It's a fake smile.

"Yes. But her psychological state..." Dr. Higgs looks at Dr. Belzan, who takes over.

"We know she experienced severe trauma. We've sent therapists to work with her. We're prepared for a psychiatric evaluation next. She refuses to speak."

"Are you sure she *can*?" Harry asks.

"Yes. She's told us so."

"That sounds circular. How could she tell you if she refuses to speak?"

"I asked her if she could, and she nodded *yes*," Dr. Belzan explains.

"Then why is she refusing to talk?"

"We don't know. Her interactivity is low. She's choosing to reduce her contact with humans as much as possible."

Dr. Belzan puts her hand on Dr. Higgs's elbow and whispers something. He nods.

"Actually, she did speak last night. One word. One of our nurse's aides was in the room after she woke up from a nightmare," Dr. Higgs says.

Monica's eyes goes wide and she asks with excitement, "What did she say?"

"The aide thinks she said the name 'Drew.'" Dr. Belzan looks at me.

121

My heart starts doing a dance in my chest, a flood of relief and warmth flowing through me.

Attagirl.

She's coming back to me.

"That's it?" Harry asks, his face carefully neutral. "Is the aide sure?"

Dr. Higgs shakes his head. "No. He's fifty-fifty on it. She was a mess when she woke up, but she opened her mouth and she tried to say something."

"Silas Gentian heard it," I interrupt.

Harry just nods.

"Has she spoken since?" Monica asks.

"No." Dr. Belzan clearly doesn't want to say that word, but she has no choice.

"Is this something we need to worry about? She was only home for a week or so after spending four years at a...at the Island," Monica whispers, eyes wide. She and Harry exchange a look that makes it clear they've already talked about the issue.

I harden inside.

I know what comes next.

"Are you thinking about sending her back?" Dr. Belzen asks.

Perceptive.

"We want what's best for Lindsay," Harry announces.

They want what's best for his presidential campaign.

I shuffle in my seat and face Monica square on. "For God's sake, you said it yourself, Monica – she'd only been home for about a week before those bastards kidnapped her, degraded her, abused her – on national television -- and worse. She was party to a murder in front of an audience of millions. We damn near lost her. Give her time to heal. At home," I say pointedly.

"I told you we shouldn't have him here," Monica says, not even bothering to lower her voice.

"So I was the savior a few days ago and now I'm a gadfly?"

"You've always been a gadfly, Drew," she responds flatly.

"You're looking for any excuse to send her back. You can't, you know."

"If she's not competent, we're her next of kin. We absolutely can."

I look at Dr. Belzan. "Is she incompetent?"

She shakes her head. "I see no signs of legal incompetence. She's capable of self care. She's just choosing not to speak."

"That's a sign of mental illness in and of itself. Who would choose not to talk when they can?" Monica insists.

"Someone who is extremely traumatized."

"If she's that traumatized, she needs intensive psychiatric help! The kind we can't give her!"

"You mean the kind you won't give her, because you've placed Harry's ambitions above your own daughter's wellbeing," I snap.

I expect to be slapped. Maybe I deserve it. Instead, Monica stands and walks out of the room. She looks back at Harry. It's clear she expects him to follow.

He doesn't.

She slams the door as she exits.

"You're right, Drew, but do you have to be so damn blunt about it? She's a grieving mother," Harry grouses. His normally commanding presence is being ground down by exhaustion.

And probably by spending so much time with Monica.

"*Grieving?* Is that the term your PR folks have decided polls best?"

His look hardens.

But he doesn't argue.

Throughout the exchanges, the doctors stay quiet. They're clearly uncomfortable.

I'm done with feeling anything.

I'm done with allowing Lindsay to be treated like a thing. A pawn. They'd be horrified by the analogy, but what Monica and Harry are doing is no different from what Nolan Corning did.

The degree of abusiveness is the only difference. It's a big one, sure.

The general principle is the same: they're all using Lindsay without any regard for her wishes.

I am the keeper of her volition.

If she has any.

I'm assuming she still does, no matter how buried it is.

I'd better be right.

My entire life hangs on the assumption that I'm right.

Which means I'm damn invested.

"Drew, we're all on the same side," Harry says with a sigh.

"I don't think that's true. I'm on Lindsay's side and you're on the Oval Office's side."

"I'm not having this argument with you." The look he gives me adds the word *again*, though he won't say it in front of the doctors. "We're her parents. We're her next of kin." He looks at Higgs, then Belzan. "At what point do we determine our next step?"

"She'll be healed enough to go home in three days or so. I'd say a psych eval in two days, and we go from there," Dr. Higgs replies. "If she does need long term inpatient psych care, they need to have physical therapy and occupational therapy rehab facilities."

Harry gives him a sour look. "Lindsay will have everything she needs."

"We're not there yet," Dr. Belzan objects. "She's getting better day by day."

"But still not speaking. Not engaging in direct eye contact," Harry confirms.

"No." Dr. Belzan's shoulders drop as she says the word.

Harry stands. "Right." He gives me a firm glare. "For now, you can have access to her. Don't engage Monica again on this, Drew. It's not black and white."

I bite my tongue. I've said what I need to say. My jaw feels like I'm biting a piece of coal hard enough to form a diamond.

I jolt.

Diamond.

I give him a conciliatory smile, relief flooding through me. "Right. You're right, Harry. It's not black and white, and I promise to be more tactful with Monica."

Surprise spreads through his features, his body language suddenly friendlier. "Glad you're coming around to see that. We all want what's best for Lindsay."

A memory from four years ago, one I've tucked away in a locked box for too long, surfaces. My coat that night, left in my car as we went to the party.

The tiny velvet box in my breast pocket.

My sister, giving me that box when I was discharged from the hospital. Calling Harry to find out Lindsay had been shipped off to the Island while I had been hospitalized.

Funny.

The color of the velvet is gray.

A plan forms, the pieces falling into place like teeth on a series of gears, lining up perfectly. "Right, Harry. There's always room for shades of gray," I declare with a smile.

We thank the doctors and walk out together, Harry splitting off before I go in to see Lindsay. As I watch his form swallowed by an elevator, I press my back against the painted cinderblock wall, breathing slowly, letting memory be my mistress for a few fabulous moments. Playful and sweet, I can become a different me when memory takes over.

Lindsay doesn't know this.

That night four years ago, I was weeks away from graduating from West Point. I was also hours away from proposing to her.

The stakes are higher now.

All my reasons for proposing are still there. If anything, I have more now. The young girl I knew then, nineteen and sheltered, has emerged a fierce woman, headstrong and brave. I'll be honored if she'll have me.

Before I ask, I have to see how close she is. I can't bridge the gap between us, but if she needs an outstretched hand, I am here.

I've always been here.

And if she'll have me, I always will.

LINDSAY

I know they're talking about me.

I know what Mom and Daddy want to do. And I won't go. My throat starts beating hard, blood racing through me, chattering like it is saying all the words I'm not.

I also know Drew will come to visit again. Every time he's here, the thin membrane between me and the world stretches a little more. I need him here. I wish he could just be with me all the time, his steady presence like an anchor.

Saying that is impossible, of course. The minute I say a single word, the dam breaks. Already, I feel like every finger, every toe, every elbow, every part of me that can is holding back leaks in the dam of emotion inside me.

Saying a word would be a sonic boom.

And the rush of water will drown me.

Tap tap tap.

I slow my breathing and turn my body slightly away from the door, knowing it's Drew. I saw him go into the conference room with Daddy and Mom and the doctors. They're all worried about me. My shoulder is healing nicely, but the nightmares won't leave.

And then there's the fact that I've disappointed Drew.

I haven't been there for him. I know how hard this has been for him. Stellan, John and Blaine released the video of their attack on Drew just as he was detained, when they kidnapped me. I know because a nurse's aide left the television on in my room and I changed the channel. Three hours of cable news and eventually you see everything.

126

They can't put me on a news blackout here. Daddy and Mom tried, I'm sure, but Dr. Belzan stepped in.

I'm sorry, I think, as Drew slowly walks into the room. He's breathing fast, the sound raspy and full. It's an emotional sound, and for some reason my skin goes hot, then cold. I'm clammy under the sheet and blanket, like I have the chills.

"Lindsay." He crosses the room quickly, his hard-soled shoes going *clack-clack-clack* in three steps, the scrape of chair legs against the tile, and then --

Oh, sweet God.

He takes my hand in his.

Other than medical personnel working on me, and a single hug from Mom and Daddy the first day I woke up, no one has touched me. All Drew does is hold his flat palm under mine. His hands are rough, hot, and dry like thick parchment paper. He places my hand, palm down, on his.

And then he waits.

Doesn't say a word.

All the words are, of course, crammed into my body, blood screaming, skin singing, bones vibrating, every part working in concert like a symphony.

And my heart is is the big bass drum.

I can't live like this.

"It's been eight days, Lindsay," he finally says, his voice measured, his words respectful and soft. "Eight days since I failed you."

I frown. No. No, you didn't.

My breath quickens, the sound like wildfire ripping across a drought-ravaged plain. Over and over, seconds tick by, the sound amplified in my ears as if it accumulates.

And still, Drew waits.

"I know where you are, baby. I know how close you are to reaching out. I know you asked for me last night."

I sigh. I freeze.

"You don't have to say a word. You don't have to do anything you don't want to do, Lindsay. I'm here when you're ready. But I have to tell you that your parents don't see it the same way. They're talking about sending you back to the Island."

I start to shake. I'm not surprised. It occurred to me, but hearing Drew say it makes it real.

"I'm not here to talk about that, though. I won't push. They might, but I won't. I am just going to sit here and when you want me, squeeze my hand. If you want me to go, push it off. That's it. A simple choice. All yours."

I open my eyes to slits, just enough to look down at my outstretched body. I feel so naked, so cold. I'm not, though. I'm warm and covered, cared for and whole.

I know I am.

But I don't *feel* like I am.

That's the problem.

They say madness is a state where you're disconnected from reality. Where the mind makes you see what isn't there.

I don't see anything unreal.

My problem is the opposite.

I can't actually see what's *really* there. Can't feel it. I've lost my emotional imagination. The colorful internal landscape of hope and dreams, of imagined realities in the future, of goals and aspirations and smiles and forward thinking is just...gone.

Like me.

I'm not here.

How can I reach for Drew if I'm not here?

Drew leans over me. He's trying to get me to open my eyes. I want to. I even will them open, but they stay shut, the impulse to open slamming against my skin, building up like a muscle spasm, releasing with a sigh. I have two selves warring inside me. Maybe more.

"Let me tell you a story." As he speaks, his warm breath fills the space between us. I smell coffee and mint. My tongue goes wet, memory a two-faced friend, as I find myself tasting him.

If I lay here and don't move, he'll go away. He has to.

But if I move, if I just reach out enough, if I confess I don't know what to do next, how to breathe next, how to be in whatever "next" is, then...what?

What will he do?

What will I do?

"Four years ago," he says in a voice that makes it clear this is the beginning of a longish tale, "I woke up in a hospital room. My mom was asleep on the chair across from my bed. It was nighttime, and I had all these tubes in me. No broken bones. Just bruises and torn...well, I was torn up." His voice drops on the last words.

He doesn't elaborate.

Doesn't need to.

"I was drugged up and dehydrated, and I panicked. Where were you? I needed to get back to you. My memory flooded, like a tsunami rushing in, like a wave of adrenaline I rode without a surfboard. It crashed into me, drowning me, and I started ripping out needles and sensors, even as the room spun." He lets out a huff of air. "In my mind, I was trying to get to you. Find you. Save you."

I hold my breath.

"Mom screamed for help and they pinned me down, shot me full of something that knocked me out. I guess I kept screaming your name. No one knew what had happened at that point – at least, my parents didn't know. The video of your – of what they did to you -- showed up later." He shifts in his chair, his hand moving slightly.

I don't squeeze.

"My sister told me you'd been sent to a 'meditation center' to recover, but I knew that was bullshit. They put you in a mental institution. Your dad sent a letter explaining that I was to have no contact with you, and if I tried, the threat was clear. Harry didn't even have to say it. He told me explicitly not to reply back, and to give my statement to investigators. I did. Never heard back."

He makes a sound that echoes with helplessness. It's so unlike him I almost open my eyes to make sure this is really Drew.

"And then I entered an emotional black hole."

I let out a big breath. Black hole. I have one of those where my soul used to be.

"It was like there was this invisible shield between the world and me. One I couldn't breach. One no one could see, but I felt it nonstop. At first, I thought it protected me."

Oh.

"I could numb out. My body healed pretty fast, Lindsay, but my heart never did. It didn't really start to heal until that day I picked you up at the Island and got you on that chopper. All that time, it was just dormant, the last part of me behind that invisible shield."

Oh.

"I hardened myself. Became a revenge machine. Developed every tactical skill I could think of. Volunteered for diplomatic missions. Saved Harry after his helicopter crash in Lagos. Learned to be a sniper. Learned how to kill. More important – learned how to protect. And for four years, I told myself it was all for you, Lindsay." he sighs. "You."

Suddenly, his warm, reassuring palm is gone. Panic flutters in my chest like a butterfly. *Wait!* I want to scream. *I wasn't ready. Give me time. I'm so close! I just need more time,* I want to plead. I even part my lips, ready to say something.

Drew stands and starts to pace. I know this because I've opened my eyes and watch him, trying to calm my body down, trying to make my ribs stop ringing.

"All those years, I was wrong."

He halts in front of me, bending slowly to eye level, his gun holster revealed, his shirt uneven across his ribs. Bandages. I realize the lumpy look comes from bandages. How badly was he hurt?

His hand covers mine again, and this time, he does squeeze.

"I wasn't preparing to protect you."

Our eyes lock.

"I was protecting *me*."

The longer he lets me just look at him, our breathing in sync, his hand holding mine, the closer I can get to him. The darkness within doesn't seem so vast. It gets smaller as I inhale, then exhale, the enormity shrinking just through the balm of time.

"I was protecting the 'me' in the past that I couldn't protect then," he elaborates. I look at his mouth, the curve of his nose, how intense his eyes get when he speaks with passion. With compassion.

With love.

"So for all those years I beat myself up. I told myself I'd never let it happen again. And then it did."

No.

"I failed you."

No!

"But worst of all, I failed myself. And when you fail yourself, you have two choices. You make it right, or you give up. Please don't give up, Lindsay. Come back to me, but come back to me because you want to. Do it for yourself. Make it right for you. I'm here. I'll be here to hold you up. Hell, if I could breathe for you, I would."

He lets out an intense sigh, his eyes darting left and right, like he's struggling. Then he looks at me again and says, "But I can't. And I won't. Because if you don't break through this for you and do it yourself, then I'll have robbed you of even more parts of yourself than have already been taken. I am not going to be that man, Lindsay. I won't take any more from you. When you're ready to connect, though, I'm here to give."

A sound comes out of me, a breathy protest from deep in my chest, like my heart needs to speak but can't figure out how. It's a sound of yielding, a quiet plea.

This is what invisible shields sound like when they give way.

CHAPTER FOURTEEN

DREW

She squeezes my hand. Her mouth tightens as her shoulders relax, her legs sinking into the mattress, her body releasing some pent-up tension I didn't know she had. Her eyes won't leave my face and that little sound she just made is the best form of *I love you* that I've ever heard.

She's looking at me, really looking. I sense a change in her. A part of me gives a victory shout, except it ricochets in my heart, coming out as a thin tremor in my hand, excitement filling me.

Lindsay is coming home.

To me.

"You didn't fail," she whispers. "I did. *I* failed."

"Oh, baby, no. No, no, you were a goddamn warrior. Always have been."

She squeezes my hand. A thousand angels sing in my head.

But there's only one angel on earth – and she's *talking* to me.

"I don't know how to be," she confesses. Emotion overwhelms me. I know that feeling.

"You don't have to be any specific way. Just let it all unroll in due course." Having her look at me, talk to me – it's sweet glory. I control my breathing because if I don't, I'll start gasping like I'm running the last mile of a marathon.

"Drew," she whispers, looking at me like my soul is hanging out of my body, "it hurts."

I look at her shoulder. "I know. I should have tackled him before the gun went off, but -- "

"Not that. Being. Being *hurts*."

"*Not* being hurts more. Because if you decide not to be, Lindsay, then they won."

She frowns.

"Every second feels like eternity." She's confessing. I'm honored.

"I know. I remember."

She gives me a sharp look, her brown eyes narrowing. "You remember? You felt it, too?"

"The black hole."

"It's worse than that," she admits. "Like -- " Her heart rate shoots up suddenly, spiking. The machine behind me starts to beep.

"Hey, hey," I soothe.

"Too much," she whispers, her voice filled with anxiety. "It's too much."

Without hesitating, I stand up, still holding her hand, and stretch out on the narrow foot or so of mattress space at the edge of the bed. She's shivering, but she doesn't tense. Doesn't freeze. Doesn't push me away.

In fact, Lindsay curls into me as much as she can, given her immobilized shoulder. Her good hand goes on my chest, finding my heart.

Like it's a guide for her own beat to follow.

Instantly, the sensors stop their crazy chatter. Lindsay's breathing settles, her eyes closed.

I'm so fucking happy.

Through the window, I see Silas's worried face. As he spots us, his face goes slack. Blank with surprise.

Then a gradual smile takes over his face and he gives me a thumb's up.

"Drew," Lindsay says, her mouth against my shoulder.

"Yes?"

"How did you get through it? The distance? The darkness?"

I shrug. "I don't know. I just did."

"No. Not good enough."

"Not good enough?"

"You don't get to avoid my question."

Jesus. I wasn't kidding when I said she was a fucking warrior. It starts to really sink in that I've chosen a woman who has brass balls when it comes to emotional issues. She expects me to be as vulnerable as I want her to be.

That's a tall order.

Only one person in my life gets to see that piece of me.

So I might as well show it to her.

Lindsay has earned it.

"Mostly revenge fantasies," I admit with a shaky sigh, hating the sound coming out of me. This is my time to be strong for her. I count the little holes in the drop ceiling panels above us, ignoring the fluorescent lights. "And being trained to kill. You know – the same way most people do."

She lets out a single laugh. "That's not funny."

"No. It's not. None of this is. I got through it by realizing I was in hell and the only way to get out of hell is to walk until you find the doorway out. Having Mark as a commanding officer helped."

"How?"

"He got it. Saw how screwed up I was. Channeled my energy."

"And the nightmares?"

I go still. How do I answer this?

With honesty. That's how.

"They don't go away. They just come less often."

She sighs, her body pressing against mine with more weight. More of the burden of just being is transferring from her to me. I take that as a sign of trust.

"How do you interact with people? I feel so..." Her voice drops off.

Tap tap tap.

She sighs before she even looks up. "Here come all the questions."

I start to climb off the bed. She clings to me.

"Don't go," she whispers urgently. "I don't want to talk to anyone but you."

I smile. I breathe. I ignore the insistent rapping on the door.

"I wish I could lay here with your forever, Lindsay. Not now, but soon."

Her grip on me tightens. "Promise?"

"I never stopped promising."

"Stay with me while they grill me?"

"Of course." I kiss the top of her head, then pull back just as Dr. Higgs walks in, eyes curious.

"Hi Lindsay," he says, giving a pregnant pause, waiting.

She looks away. "Hi," she whispers, squeezing my hand.

So hard she'll turn it into a diamond. Soon.

LINDSAY

This is the part where I'm supposed to snap out of it, let Drew kiss me madly, and we ride off into the sunset to make passionate love on the beach or in a remote cabin in the woods, the stars twinkling in the sky as we consecrate our love.

Instead, I'm getting my blood pressure checked and the doctor says, "Open your mouth and cough for me."

How romantic.

The doctor tries to make Drew move, but I've got a vise grip on his hand. He is my rock. He is my anchor. I reached out and he was there and I didn't keep falling into the eternal vacuum of nothingness.

I'm here.

I'm still here, and it's all because of him.

And me.

Me.

"Lindsay, can you say something?' Dr. Higgs asks, his eyes kind but searching.

"Something," I respond.

He laughs. Drew joins him.

"You know where you are? The year? Your birth date?"

"Yes."

"And you want Drew here with you?"

"God, yes."

He nods. "Okay, then. By now, someone on your security team has contacted your parents. I'm sure they'll be here shortly."

I groan.

"Vocal cords back to normal," Drew jokes.

I look at the doctor. "I do not need to go back to the mental institution."

He looks uncomfortable. "You knew about that?"

"I know my parents. I know how they think." My voice cracks on the last word. I haven't spoken for eight days, so I'm a little rusty. Drew lets go of my hand, grabs a pitcher, and pours me a cup of water. I sip it, grateful.

I can't grab his hand and drink at the same time, so I hurry. Not holding his hand makes me feel weightless.

Like I'll drift back off.

I don't want that.

A gnawing sensation grows inside me. The room feels big, cold, impossibly empty and clinical. I check my body again. Clothed in a hospital gown, my bad shoulder bare but bandaged.

Bedsheets and blankets cover the rest of me.

The nightmares leave me naked and bereft, the line between reality and dream so thin, so fragile.

Drew's strong hand takes mine without comment.

The gnawing abates.

Dr. Higgs seems troubled by my words, the pensive look on his face remaining. "You're twenty-two, yes?"

"Twenty-three next week," Drew adds. He swallows, then smiles. "We'll have to celebrate in a special way."

Too much.

Too much to imagine. The room starts to spin, my emotions turning an invisible wheel around and around, like I'm a Merry-go-Round and his words are a source of power.

137

"Sorry," he adds in a low voice, squeezing my hand. "Let's talk about something else."

"Is it that obvious?" I ask.

"Your face turned the color of milk when I said that."

"I can't think about anything but the next few seconds."

"Got it."

The way he says it makes me believe him.

Dr. Higgs scribbles a few more notes, then gives me an evaluative look, a sigh of contemplation escaping. He crosses his arms, the chart still in his left hand, and he looks at me.

"Lindsay, we have a full psych eval scheduled for you tomorrow. We didn't know when you would start to communicate, so..."

"It's fine," I say. I don't look at him. "I can talk to them."

This pleases him.

For a moment, I feel like I'm talking to Stacia. I cringe at the thought.

"Good." He smiles. "Welcome back."

Welcome back.

He leaves. Drew lays down next to me again, this time on his side, his hand caressing my face. I let him.

I like it.

But it's so hard to look at him. Intensity radiates out from those sharp brown eyes, gone to a deep, rich chocolate swirling with emotion. I know he's spent eight days holding back.

I've spent eight days finding my way back.

"If this is too much -- "

I turn to him. "It's fine. I – it's a little unreal."

"I know."

"I can't stop feeling naked all the time."

"Is that why you did a body check when the doctor was here?"

"Body check?"

"You looked at yourself. Looked down. Like in a dream, where you realize you're naked in public."

"You have those dreams?"

"Everyone has those dreams, Lindsay." His face softens, going sad. "And after what you went through with the live feed in Tiffany's apartment and being on all the major cable channels like that, in the middle of trauma in a life-or-death situation, I'd be surprised if you weren't constantly body checking. Your brain has to weed out the stress imprint from what happened. It'll take time,"

I am so tired. A yawn escapes me. He doesn't react.

"I keep having this nightmare," I say, surprising myself. Sharing the weird dreams isn't what I want to do. Not consciously, at least. I guess a different part of me has taken the internal steering wheel.

"About being naked in public?" he asks.

"More than that. You're in the dream. I'm on this stage -- "

"And I'm in the audience," he chokes out, astonishment lighting his features.

I jolt. "Yes."

"How did you know?" we say in unison.

The bleak blanket that has been my only source of warmth and comfort, the heavy, weighted cloth that I've carried as a burden these days, turns to lightweight down, to sunshine in woven form, featherlight and exquisite.

"Drew? What did you say at the end of the dream? When you picked up your phone?" I beg, my voice desperate, my plea profound.

His mouth trembles with emotion, his eyes big and loving.

"I said, 'She's back. Lindsay is back.'"

CHAPTER FIFTEEN

DREW

We just let time do its thing for a few minutes. As I stare at her, unblinking, my face muscles relax. My eyes narrow. The meaning behind it all doesn't matter any longer.

The insanity of the past two weeks fades as Lindsay's features come into true focus, sharp and acute, diffuse and ethereal. I hold my space, knowing she needs hers.

She rotates in the bed, sitting up slightly, and leans in toward me. I'm still holding her hand.

"Can you forgive me?" she asks.

She might as well have slapped me.

"For what?"

"For not trusting you. For turning into an animal with them. For doing unspeakable acts in your apartment as I tried to survive. For lying to you. For -- "

I gently press my fingers against her lips, avoiding the big spot where her face is streaked with a laceration, a long red line that still looks angry.

"No. I won't forgive you."

Trepidation fills her face.

"Because there is nothing to forgive. You did what you needed to do to protect your own wholeness, Lindsay. No one ever needs to apologize for that."

"But I -- "

"In fact, I'd be disappointed if you didn't do all those things."

"Let me finish!" Her eyes shine with tears, her voice still off-kilter, scratchy. "I know I don't *need* your forgiveness, Drew. I *want* it."

When too much emotion hits me at once, I wall it off. Human beings only have so much capacity for processing. For action. For reaction.

My instinct is to retreat.

I have to override instinct and remain. Be in the present moment.

Show up.

"Then I need to ask for the same from you, Lindsay. Will *you* forgive *me*?"

She nods once, tears spilling over her lower eyelids, the drops rolling down, magnifying the plethora of healing cuts and scrapes across her beautiful, beautiful face.

"I do."

Oh, those words.

"And I do, too, baby." I want to reach for her, pull her into my arms and hold her forever. The space between us narrows, emotion deepening.

"Come here," she beckons, her good hand patting the space on the bed. She shifts as much as she can, then wipes her tears from her face, wincing. "Be close to me. Be as close as you can."

I comply. That's the best order anyone has ever given me.

And good soldiers obey good orders.

Awkward and clumsy, we twist and turn, trying to find a good way to lay in each other's arms. She snort-giggles, I sigh in frustration, and our faces bump against each other, the lightest brush of nose against nose, until suddenly I'm tasting her, and Lindsay's good hand is on my jacket lapel, clutching it hard.

No kiss has ever been so needed. No kiss has ever tasted so divine. No kiss has ever bridged so many miles, too many traumas. I want to let her lead the way but desire clings to me like her hand and I give in. My body moves against hers. She's pressing into me, her mouth eager but careful. Soon we're lost in the swirling vortex of each other. Giving into the dizzy divine is a relief.

No restraint.

No walls.

No shields.

Just *us*.

Lindsay pulls back with a tiny cry and holds her fingers up to her swollen lip. Her eyes are an apology. "Sorry. It split." She gives me a crooked grin, then just looks at me with raw tenderness, vulnerable and real. I hate the torn lip. I hate the bruises. I hate that her face looks like a calico cat, orange and yellow, mottled – yet her eyes glow with an alert love that I hope I'm sending back to her, amplified.

I brush her hair off her forehead and smile right back, blood racing, heart strong and true.

"She's back," I whisper, low and sincere. "Lindsay is back."

CHAPTER SIXTEEN

DREW

Lindsay and I are standing outside Harry's office, about to go in for the monster of all debriefings. So is Monica, along with Silas and Mark Paulson. The hospital discharged Lindsay yesterday and we spent a quiet night at her house. Monica and Harry were in D.C. I slept in Lindsay's bed, just holding her.

Neither one of us had nightmares.

Harry's public relations strategist, Marshall, is in the meeting. And, of course, two guys with faces made of putty who could be anyone and no one at the blink of an eye.

Lindsay reaches for my hand for support – needing it, offering it? Who cares. The difference doesn't matter. She eyes a tray of pastries in front of Monica.

We walk into the room, all eyes on our linked hands. I don't blame them. Between my broken finger and Lindsay's sling, we're a sight.

The first person I stare at is Marshall.

He looks away.

Not a single piece of paper is in the room. The curtains are drawn, and Marshall has a projector with a USB drive attached to it. Silas will be given the USB drive after this meeting, then he'll be put on a plane for D.C.

Nothing we're learning isn't common knowledge to a certain level of insiders in power.

But just in case...

Mark and I share a look that is nonverbal bureau-speak.

We'll talk later. He's already explained most of the basics to me behind the scenes. So basic there's really just one concept to remember: I was set up. Disentangling that will be a mess, but it's a manageable mess, especially with his help.

Lindsay and I settle into our seats. Her fingers entwine in mine, our hands resting on my right thigh. Her bad arm is in a sling, the bullet doing its damage but nature taking its course. Young and strong, in great shape and determined, Lindsay will have a full recovery. The doctors said so.

And I'll make sure it happens.

On her right sits her mother, who is as stone faced as the woman can get. It's anger, not Botox, driving the look.

"Let's start. Anya has cleared my schedule -- "

Monica shoots Harry a nasty look.

He seems bewildered, blindsided, like a little boy who can't find his pet. "Er, I mean Celia, my new assistant, has cleared my schedule for as long as this meeting takes." He cocks an eyebrow at me. "And I suspect that will be a very long time."

"Let's hear Marshall first. I'll fill in the details afterward, and Paulson and Gentian can give more, too," I reply.

"What about Jane?" Lindsay asks. "She should be here."

"That conniving little liar?" Monica huffs. "Absolutely not." Monica wears an all-cream suit with a pleated wool skirt, gold piping matching her earrings, bracelets and necklace. Her hair has recently been colored, the cut and style capable of remaining intact in an F-5 tornado.

She looks like a wall of anger.

"I suggested it. She's been cleared of everything but hacking charges, and once she testifies against Nolan Corning and his minions, she'll be cleared," Marshall says to my surprise. I have to give him a sliver of grudging credit.

A sliver.

"It wasn't her fault. Wasn't Anya's, either," Lindsay says, her voice trailing off as she frowns, clearly still processing the emotional fallout.

Monica reaches for Lindsay's good shoulder, eyes blazing in contrast to the compassion in her voice. "You're very kind to worry about your friend, but she betrayed you. Double-crossed everyone. Put your father's campaign in jeopardy and your life in danger."

Notice the priority in that sentence?

"So did her disgusting, traitorous mother," Monica adds.

Harry looks like someone just kicked him in the balls.

Lindsay's taken aback by her mother's ferocity. "Jane didn't have a choice, Mom. They basically kidnapped her."

"She fed them information about you. Anya handed you off to those *pigs*." Monica's eyes crawl over Lindsay's face and upper body, inventorying in a very obvious way, punctuating the severity of her remarks.

"Because she was protecting Jane!" Lindsay protests.

"Don't you dare defend that bitch!" Monica hisses, red-faced and livid, jumping to her feet and leaning in. She and Lindsay are inches from each other, their chests heaving, the scent of Monica's custom-blended perfume rising off her like distorted heat waves on southern California asphalt in July.

"That 'bitch' was my assistant for most of my political career!" Harry roars, recovering from Monica's vengeful dominance. All eyes turn to him, through Monica is slower. "Anya was not a traitor. She did what she did because Corning's men threatened Jane's life. She came to me as soon as she could."

"Not good enough, Harry," Monica replies. It occurs to me that there is something much deeper going on regarding Monica's feelings for Anya. This isn't just about Lindsay.

This is a grudge match.

"It's good enough for me. Anya's never working for me again. Her career in political administration is destroyed. Her daughter may face federal hacking charges and their lives are ruined. That doesn't erase the good work she did for me for years, and not one damn iota of this conversation has anything to do with moving on and finding a way to come out of this mess on top," Harry announces.

Marshall clears his throat. "Moving on, then…"

Monica makes a sound deep in her throat that makes it clear she has *not* moved on.

Lindsay bites back a smile and squeezes my hand.

"Here are the facts as we know them," Marshall says, looking across the table at Mark Paulson. "Four years ago, Nolan Corning created an exploratory committee to look into running for president. By the time the committee was done, they honed in on their biggest obstacle: Senator Harwell Bosworth."

Lindsay's smile fades.

"Corning and Harry clashed – hard – over the years within the party, but Harry had no reason to believe Corning was capable of what he eventually ordered." Marshall appears to fumble for words.

"You mean no one would have guessed he was evil enough to hire three of my friends to rape and torture Lindsay for political gain," I clarify.

Monica's eyes dart to me. Harry sighs.

Silas and Mark remain stonefaced.

"You could put it that way," Marshall says in a terse voice.

"I just did."

Lindsay squeezes my hand. "But how did he do it? How did he get those three guys in particular? They went to school with Drew, he knew them much of his life," Lindsay asks.

The ten million dollar question.

Why Lindsay? Why the gang rape on streaming television? Why such an outrageous act?

"Corning is sealed tight. However, some extraneous information -- "

A euphemism for hacking.

" -- reveals that the initial contact was with Blaine Maisri. We've found significant sums of money that were channeled through subsidiary accounts connected to Corning supporters and funneled into businesses owned by the Maisri family, but the forensic research on this will take a very long time to unravel."

"Could you translate that into English?" Lindsay asks.

"Corning paid Maisri off," Marshall says sourly, not looking at her.

"So those assholes got paid to rape me," she replies.

Marshall, Harry and Monica flinch.

"Among other things," I add. "The meteoric rise of Blaine, Stellan and John in their respective careers must have been part of the deal, too."

"If the goal was to humiliate Daddy by using me, then..." Lindsay falters. "I don't know." She shakes her head.

"Say it," Monica whispers. "Go ahead. Today is the day to just get all this shit out so we can move on."

"Did they have to be so vicious about it? So sadistic?" Lindsay takes in a long, shaky breath. "And video it?"

"That was all part of the plan, according to some of the communication we've intercepted," Marshall explains. "It needed to be such a scandal that it would dominate headlines. The specific goal was to paint you as an out-of-control slut -- "

"But -- "

"There's more," Marshall says, holding up his hand, pausing Lindsay. "And to distract the mainstream media while Corning shoved through a massive appropriations bill that contained ethically-questionable riders."

Harry reels back. "He what?"

Monica's eyes turn to angry slits. "He used Lindsay's scandal to distract the country, and Harry, so he could push legislation through Congress?"

"Yes," Marshall confirms. "It was a massive distraction."

Harry lets out a colorful ribbon of expletives.

Monica gives a bitter laugh. "Your father's approval ratings have soared since the story came out about Nolan Corning!" Monica gushes, her voice a strange brew of over-the-top enthusiasm and stark fury. "This has been absolutely fabulous for his campaign."

"Glad to be of help," Lindsay mutters.

I explode.

LINDSAY

I am not used to having my own cheering section 24/7. He's holding my hand and screaming at my mother. No one ever mentioned that when you fall in love, this constant defender comes with the territory.

I like it.

"No matter how many times I tell myself you have more depth, you find a way to disprove it, Monica! Jesus Fucking Christ, no one cares about Harry's approval ratings!" Drew shouts.

Daddy and Marshall interrupt him, saying, "Actually, we do," both at the same time.

"Not at Lindsay's expense!" Drew snaps.

Mom looks like he called her a bad name.

"I would never put Harry's campaigns above Lindsay's best interests!" she retorts in a haughty voice, clutching the gold necklace she's wearing.

I start laughing. I can't stop. One look at Silas tells me he's trying not to laugh. Drew is red-faced and puffed up, livid on my behalf, and can't calm down enough to giggle at the absurdity that just came out of my mother's mouth.

"When have you ever – even once! -- put Lindsay ahead of your political ambitions?" Drew yells at her, getting in Mom's face. She actually leans way back, afraid.

And then her cunning nature kicks in.

"*My* political ambitions?" She wags a finger at him. It's perfectly manicured, the French tip flawlessly drawn. "*My* political ambitions? Oh, no. You do not get to lecture me about political ambition – this is all for Harry."

Daddy snorts.

Mom turns on him, murderous.

"Don't even go there."

His face goes slack.

"Could we get back to the topic at hand..." Marshall implores, clearing his throat again. "We have a great deal of ground to cover."

"And Lindsay has her psych eval for the Island in ninety minutes," Mom adds in a matter-of-fact tone.

I clasp Drew's elbow, mostly to get his attention, but partly to make sure he doesn't haul off and punch my mother.

"The Island?" I challenge. "I'm not being evaluated to go to the Island. I'm just being checked out to make sure I'm okay."

Marshall and Mom share a look.

I know that look.

No. Fucking. Way.

"I am not going to the Island," I announce, mustering as much authority as I can. "They did an eval before they let me go yesterday. This is just a follow-up. I have to get my wounds re-bandaged, too. It's all a formality."

Daddy shoves a stack of newspapers across the conference table. The top one, a color tabloid, has full-body shots of me in Tiffany's living room, naked and shoving a knife in Stellan's crotch. My breasts and mons are blurred out.

"These are everywhere, sweetie," Daddy explains, not looking at me. "This isn't going away. We're just replacing one scandal with another. And you...well, you killed someone. The psych evaluations are necessary. And Stacia says -- "

"The police cleared me of all charges. I'm free to do whatever I need as long as I give them my contact information for interviews and investigations. No one is questioning that what I did to Stellan was self-defense," I say, anger burning through my body.

"And well deserved," Drew chimes in.

"But Stacia thinks that the trauma -- "

"I don't care what Stacia says," I respond, smooth as silk as I cut off Mom's words. "I am almost twenty-three years old and I am a legal adult. You can't make me go back to the Island against my will."

"We're your next of kin, Lindsay. And if the psychiatrist says you're not quite stable, a few weeks at the Island – just until the story and the video loops die down – might be good for you," Mom says with urgency. "I would love two or three weeks on an island recuperating," she adds with a titter than makes me want to punch her in the throat.

Now Drew is holding *my* elbow nice and tight.

"I'll fight you," I say through gritted teeth. "You want that all over the newspapers? 'Presidential candidate's daughter unfairly institutionalized by overbearing parents – news at 11!'"

Marshall cuts me a cold look. "Won't work. Our spin machine can paint you to look like a hysterical loon in under six hours, Lindsay."

"HEY!" Drew snaps, moving so Marshall has no line of sight on me. "That's *enough*!"

"Indeed," Daddy says in a slow, tired voice.

"Lindsay isn't going anywhere she doesn't want to go," Drew adds.

"The doctor will be the judge of that," Mom says primly.

"You can't do this," I whisper. The fight is draining out of me. I'm tired. So tired. "Why are you doing this to me?' I ask Mom, the words eerily familiar. I'm triggered, remembering John and Stellan, tasting the hot garlic in their mouths, fighting to breathe.

I'm naked Lindsay on that tabloid cover, wearing another man's blood and holding all the sins in the world in my hand.

Drew senses it, standing, slowly guiding me up. "We're done," he announces. Silas stands, loyal to Drew. Mark Paulson stays seated. His eyes are on Daddy.

Mom pretends nothing negative has been said, as if their plan to send me to the Island is a gift. "Tired? Oh, sweetie, go rest. Maybe your discharge came a bit too early." She gives me a long look.

She's not talking about yesterday's discharge from the hospital.

She's talking about my discharge from the Island, weeks ago.

As Drew guides me out the door he and Mark share a look.

"We'll talk later," Drew says to him. Mark just nods and gives me a sympathetic smile.

"Thank you," I say to him, the words inadequate.

"Any time," he says. I know he means it. Mark stays in the room as Marshall resumes his debriefing.

I heard what I needed to hear.

CHAPTER SEVENTEEN

DREW

Rule number one when dealing with a determined, empowered enemy: run.

It's the same first response we recommend to civilians in active shooter settings, too.

"So Mom and Daddy still want to ship me off to the Island until the media storm is over, Jane and Anya turned on me but for good reasons, Jane actually didn't turn on me because she's my darknet informant and used hacking skills to get the secret videotape that proves my innocence...and I forgot to grab one of those apple fritters back there on the table!" Lindsay's stomach growls like an exclamation point at the end of her rant. "Another way to get back and Mom – eat carbs in front of her!"

I chuckle in spite of my fury. "Let's fix one of those. Getting you a pastry is the easy part," I say, carefully wrapping my arm around her shoulders as we walk slowly to the parking garage.

"You are bright red, hot as hell, and your heart is zooming," she tells me as we walk, holding tight.

"Hot as hell? Love the compliment, baby."

"I mean from screaming at my mom," she says with a soft laugh. "But yeah. You're hot no matter what."

Flirting. Lindsay is *flirting*.

She's not even close to being one hundred percent, but then again, neither am I. We have healing – inside and out-- and time is our best form of medicine.

Time together, that is.

As we get to the elevators for the parking garage, I

press the lobby button. Her face screws up in confusion.

"I thought we were leaving."

"Let's walk down the street to a bakery."

She smiles shyly and says nothing, stepping onto the elevator as the doors open. We're alone on the ride down. I hold her close, mind churning, careful not to hurt her shoulder.

My coat contains something special, right in the same inner breast pocket where the crown of her head touches.

But she doesn't know.

We're both deep in our own thoughts, the elevator bell *ding!* startling us, making Lindsay smile and shake her head. The sun is blinding, like always. It's good to know the world goes on even as our own individual worlds seemed to fall apart for a little while.

Time to put life back together, better than ever.

"Are you okay?" Lindsay asks, pausing. I stop walking and look at her, my gut clenching.

In the sunlight, she's more beaten up. Hospital lighting is harsh, but sunlight is the great equalizer. She must see something in my face, some part of my reaction I can't hide, because she reaches up and touches her hair.

"I'm fine." I mimic her, except instead of touching my hair, I pat my pocket. The little velvet box is in there, along with an important envelope.

Last night was a long night at Lindsay's place. While she slept, insomnia gripped me. A man can do a lot of thinking in his girlfriend's bed, her light breath warming his arm, her gorgeous self in a state of total trust.

A *lot* of thinking.

I have a plan.

A harmless little plan of my own.

We find a small cafe. I guide her to a private table, then go to the counter and return with two coffees and a box of assorted pastries. Lindsay peeks in the box and laughs.

"Planning a party? Who do you expect to eat all this, Drew? There's enough for a dozen people."

I admire the curve of her arm as she reaches up to

brush her hair back from her face. She grabs an apple pastry and takes a bite, groaning with culinary pleasure.

I enjoy that, too.

As we steal these peaceful moments from the rest of our tumultuous lives, I wait. I know she'll bring it up.

And finally, she does.

"Do you really think they'll try to send me to the Island?"

"Yes."

"I won't go."

"Then don't."

"They have so much power, Drew. You know them. They'll find a way if they really want me gone."

My body goes tight with a protective streak I've had since the day I met her. "We can stop them."

"How?"

It's suddenly very warm in this little cafe. Sweat breaks out where my collar meets my neck. I rub my palms on the tops of my thighs.

You can do this, Foster.

I can take out an Afghan warlord from hundreds of yards away, cool as a cucumber and steady as can be with a rifle and not break a sweat.

But the thought of asking Lindsay to marry me makes me overheat.

Yeah, *marry*.

"I have an idea."

"Bring it on," she says, her good arm waving with encouragement before she picks up her coffee and drinks some.

"Your parents keep holding the fact that they are your next of kin over your head." I start to fidget. I hate fidgeting. My right leg bounces up and down like an eager puppy with a fetch stick in its mouth.

"Right."

"What if you could change that?"

"Like, pick someone to have medical power of attorney over me? I think Daddy and Mom would -- "

"No, I mean change your next of kin."

"Drew, I don't understand." Her eyes are wide and searching my face. I haven't connected the dots for her. My heart crawls into my throat, resting there, needing a short pause before making the final journey to the summit of Mount Ask Lindsay to Marry Me.

Fortifying myself with a few gulps of coffee, I drain my cup, set it on the table, then take her good hand in mine.

"I think you should marry me, Lindsay."

LINDSAY

"Did you just *propose*?" I did not hear that. I didn't.

"Yes."

I did hear it.

He *did*.

He said that. He said he wants to *marry* me.

"No," I blurt out. Moving my hand breaks contact with him. I feel a wide wedge between us, getting bigger.

"No?"

"I mean, yes!"

"No or yes, Lindsay. There are two options and you've used them both within seconds of each other." Is that sweat on his forehead? Drew doesn't get nervous. Oh, my God is he *nervous*?

"No! I mean, yes! No, I mean, I don't want you to marry me out of pity or because you want to win."

"Win? Marrying you would be the best kind of win."

"I'm not some trophy! Or a prize you get for outsmarting my parents!"

He's stunned. "You think *that's* why I proposed?" Drew's arms cross over his chest, his chin tipped down, looking up at me under thick lashes, giving me a questioning look so smoldering all I want to do is kiss him.

I shrug instead.

This really befuddled look pours through his face like a rainfall of emotion. Drew is so stoic most of the time – hell, *all* of the time – that it's almost comical.

158

I laugh, anyhow, and then I start to cry softly. Salt in my tears makes all the cuts on my face sting.

"Let me do this properly," he announces, reaching into his breast pocket of his jacket. What's he doing? He couldn't possibly have a --

A ring?

A tiny gray velvet box is in his hand, and he flicks it open with his thumb like it's a lighter and he's starting a flame.

Which he is.

Only with a diamond.

My mouth drops open. "Drew!" I gasp. "I saw this on your nightstand table that day. I remember. It was next to that ridiculous book about airplanes -- " I clap both hands over my own mouth to stop the stupid from pouring out of me.

He drops to one knee.

Oh, my GOD.

"I said I needed to do this properly."

"You came prepared," I squeak through my open fingers.

"I came determined to win." He reaches for my hand. "To win your heart, Lindsay. Forever."

You ever realize that the world just continues marching on, second by second, regardless of your internal emotional state? That's how it feels, breathing. Drew is on one knee. His hands are held out to me. One hand holds a box with a diamond ring in it, marquis cut, glittering like his eyes. Shining with love.

He's begging me with those eyes. All of the love in the world is centered on me right now.

And I can't breathe.

I'm holding my breath for all the good reasons. Every damn one of them. This is what joy feels like. This is what hope feels like.

I've known love. I've known happiness. I've known contentment, though only in slivers.

But *joy*? Joy has been elusive. It has been forced into hiding for so very long it's not sure that there's a safe place to come out.

Drew, before me, makes that safe space. It's the air between us. It's the look he's giving me right now.

Pure joy.

Joy releases us. It gives us room. The sense of power that comes from being vulnerable cannot be measured. Joy lets us be our true self. Joy doesn't judge.

And joy is right here, smiling at us both, telling me to say *yes*.

When joy gives you a suggestion – you listen.

"Yes," I say, the word long and sweet, like the sun lives inside me and I'm opening my mouth to spread the light of love. Drew's eyes glisten – he's not crying, but now I am – and he takes my hand, so solemnly.

The ring slides up, over the knuckle of the left ring finger, settling in like it's been there forever.

This is the part where people kiss, right? Where we hug and he picks me up and twirls me around in the air.

Where we breathe in each other's fire and breathe out shared passion. Zeal. Zest for a life well lived for the next sixty years.

Right?

Instead, we're deliberate. Achingly authentic every microsecond. Drew and I know the long, horrible road we've traveled to reach this point.

A point I didn't see coming.

"I'll marry you. We -- " I'm about to say we have to tell Mom and Daddy, but given their plans for me, I'm not sure we should.

"That's the part where we both win, Lindsay," Drew explains, his grin widening. I didn't think it possibly could, but it does. "We're getting married now."

"Now?"

"Today."

"TODAY?"

"Yes."

"We can't get married today! We have to tell Mom and Daddy..." I frown.

"Baby, you know exactly what they'll do."

I halt. "They'll stop us."

"Yes."

"And try to send me back to the Island."

"I won't let that happen." He leans in and plants a gentle kiss on my lips. "But marrying me today can make damn sure they can't control you any longer."

"You want to marry me so *you* can control me?"

"I want to marry you so I can make love to you."

"Nice try."

"What? I do."

"We don't have to get married to do that! Let's stick to the topic at hand." Sex has been the last thing on my mind, frankly.

Suddenly, it's right there.

"But if we're married, your parents can't have any legal control over you any more. They're not your next of kin. I am."

Next of kin.

"So you're saying that getting married today would take away power from my dad and mom?"

"Yes."

I punch him. Then I kiss him, a long, wet, slow inventory that I hope shares all the dirty little ways I want to make love with him, someday, forever and ever.

"But -- " I say as our mouths separate.

He sighs.

"I told you it's a harmless little plan." He can't say the words without smiling.

I snort. "You are crazy."

"You'll do it?" He grabs my hands and holds them in front of me like we're already taking vows. "Marry me?"

I nod. "But I won't obey you."

His mouth twitches with amusement. "When have you ever?"

"You really are serious. Get married today? How?"

"Do you know where your birth certificate is?"

"No." Somewhere in a filing cabinet at The Grove, I suspect.

He reaches into his breast coat pocket again, holding

161

up an envelope, wiggling it like a fan. "I do."

"You *stole* my birth certificate from The Grove?"

"'Stole' is such a judgmental term," he says dryly.

"It's a true term!"

He pretends to be philosophical, pressing his fingers against his chin like Freud. "What, exactly, is 'truth'?"

"The truth is that I love you."

"Now we're getting somewhere."

"And your insane scheme to marry me is *brilliant*!"

"I know."

"So let's do it."

"Really?"

"You've always said you were a man of action. Prove it."

"Is that a challenge?"

"Worse."

"Worse?"

"It's a dare."

The growl from his throat sets my heart beating faster. "Do you," he whispers, pulling me in hard against his hot body, "have any idea what hearing the word 'dare' from your mouth does to me?"

"Show me."

His throat moves as he swallows, eyes half-hooded and dark. "Let's go back to my place and I'll show you."

I wince at the thought of going back there.

"No," I say between kisses. "I have a better idea."

He pulls back and gives me an evaluative look. He's reading my mind. I let him.

"Let's do it, then. Get married," he says, nodding.

"Where?"

"Where else?"

"Vegas," we say in unison.

CHAPTER EIGHTEEN

DREW

This isn't how I envisioned our wedding, but I'm a realist.

And realistically, it was going to be a long shot that I could pull this off without Harry and Monica learning about our plans.

If anyone can do it, though, it's me.

In the life we were supposed to have, our wedding would have been a society affair, me in dress uniform, a thousand or more politically-connected guests present at The Grove in an extravaganza the media would cover.

In the life we were supposed to have, my parents wouldn't be dead – likely killed by Nolan Corning's machine, it turns out, for reasons Mark and I are still trying to discover – and my sister, brother-in-law, and toddler nephew would be there, cheering us on.

In the life we were supposed to have, Lindsay wouldn't be recovering from a gunshot wound as we drive to Vegas to escape her self-centered, oppressive parents.

But we don't get to choose what life does to us.

Only how we react to it.

As we drive across the desert through the long stretch to Las Vegas, Lindsay stares out the window, sunlight playing on the shadow of scars that mark her cheekbone. I can't remove those. Can't even cover them up. All I can do is use them as a reminder of a time when I had no power.

A time now long in the past. I will never be in the same position again.

And neither will Lindsay.

I know she thinks I asked her to marry her for all the wrong reasons.

What she doesn't understand is that four years ago, I had this ring in my pocket. It was in my coat, outside in my car that night of the party. I'd planned to propose then.

All I did today was to right a wrong.

The *final* wrong.

And now it's all right. Everything's right.

Everything is *perfect*.

She spins the diamond around and around on her finger, the wind pushing through the open windows, her body as relaxed as it can be with her arm in a sling.

Lindsay turns to me and gives me a pensive look. "There's one thing you should know before we get married, Drew."

"What's that?"

"I don't want to sleep with you."

"Ever?" I feel like someone just threw a brick at my balls.

"No. No, no, no – not ever! No. I mean, someday. Of course I do. Maybe *want* is the wrong word. How about *can't*? Or...not yet? I just..." She blinks hard. Her throat tightens, then moves with effort. Whatever's going on inside her over this, she's trying to communicate – and it's hard for her. I can't do anything that makes her trust me less.

But this is not your typical road trip conversation when you're on your way to get married, is it?

"Hey. Hey. It's okay, Lindsay. I'll wait. You're worth it. We're worth it." That's the best I can come up with on the fly.

It seems to calm her down.

"I guess I'm trying to manage expectations. I'm overanalyzing, aren't I? I do that a lot these days." She raises the window and re-positions the air conditioning vents. I raise my window and the sound difference is enormous. We're suddenly in a cocoon. It feels intimate.

It *is* intimate.

This is life.

"Do you really want to talk about sex right now?"

Her pause makes it hard for me not to smile.

"Yes," she admits.

"Then let's do it – talk, I mean," I add in a rush. "Talk. Not do."

"Are you as awkward as I am?" she asks seriously. "I feel like I need to be open about this."

"That's what we're doing, Lindsay. Being real. Being open."

"Okay." She takes in a resolved breath. "Then I'll be open. I want to have sex. I'm angry I haven't been having sex. I'm just so angry about everything! And then I imagine having sex and I want to die."

I was with her right up to that last sentence.

"Sex makes you think about dying?"

"Not sex with you."

"Thinking about sex with other men makes you want to die?" This conversation makes me irrationally angry.

"Thinking about what happened in your apartment does."

"Got it." I calm down.

"I can see I'm upsetting you. I'll stop talking about it."

"No," I say softly. "Yes, it upsets me. But it would upset me more if you felt like you couldn't share parts of the true you with me. I'm here. I'm here to listen. I'm here to touch and heal with. Only when you're ready, though."

"That's what makes this so hard!" she says, her body vibrating with frustration. "You're patient and understanding and calm and rational and so damn perfect!"

"And that's...bad?" Women. I really, really do not understand her.

"It is when I'm such a mess."

I sigh and run a hand through my hair. My fingertips are ice cold. "I'm a mess, too," I admit.

"You are?"

I nod.

"How?"

"I think it would be easier to tell you all the ways I'm *not* a mess."

Her eyes light up. "That's how I feel, too."

"But no one shot me. No one made me parade naked in a room full of people – and on streaming television, covered by every major cable news channel, replayed over and over, still in the newspapers even now. No one violated me the way those animals did to you, Lindsay. I'm not trying to compare what I'm feeling to what you're feeling -- "

"That's just it, Drew – you *can*!" Her breathing goes shallow, her chest rising and falling, the conversation stressing her out. I want to tell her to stop, but this feels pivotal. We have two more hours to get to Vegas and it feels like this topic is the answer to the meaning of life.

"I would never try to compare."

"I am not some special tortured snowflake! Don't do this to me, too. Everyone's walking around on eggshells with me. Do you know how alone I feel? How lonely? How different and unique? Those words really, really isolate. They turn me into some freak again. Unreachable and misunderstood. I can't have you do that, too, Drew. Not you." She starts sobbing, her chin tucked into her chest at an awkward angle.

How did we get from the topic of sex to *this*?

Doesn't matter. I can't continue driving while she's crying, pouring her heart out to me. I pull over, the tires rolling gently to a stop. Within seconds I'm across the gear shift, holding her any way I can without hurting her more.

"I'm such a m-m-mess that I'm in the car, telling you I can't have sex and crying about it as we're on our way to get married!" Lindsay says, incredulous. She looks at me with red-rimmed eyes and a wild expression. "Why in the hell would you even want to marry me?"

I kiss her. In the kiss, I pour out my heart, my soul, my anger, all the feelings that make up the impossible answer to her impossible question.

The kiss has to give her a proper response to her eternal *why?*, and as seconds pass, our lips sweetly slant against each other, my tongue parting her open to say *Yes, I love you.*

To say *We'll be a mess together.*

To say *I'll take you however you'll give yourself.*

To say *I do, forever.*

By the time the kiss ends we're breathless. I taste her tears in my mouth.

I also taste her surprise.

"I love *you*. I want *you*. The real you. Not just your good parts. Not just your unmessy self, Lindsay. I want it all. I need it all. I don't need you whole, but I need the whole *you*. Can you trust me with that much of yourself? Because I think that's how this goes. I don't know, because this is all new for me, too. But don't ever think that I love you one iota less for showing me all of your moments, dark and light," I tell her.

"You mean that? Really?"

"I do."

She's breathing hard, color in her cheeks, a pink arousal in her skin and an intense look in her eyes that I swear is passion. She's coming back into focus, the old Lindsay slowly emerging from the dark internal cave where she's been hiding, waiting for it to be safe to emerge.

That's my job.

To love her and make it safe.

"Four years ago, I knew I loved you, Drew. By it was an immature love. A surface love. Love was defined by our friends, by Mom and Daddy's approval, by dinners with your parents and by all the trappings of society and the media. I knew I loved you because we held hands, we exchanged gifts, we went to parties together, we became one word – *LindsayandDrew* – and because we were a couple who were a sum of all those parts."

I just listen.

That's my job, too.

"But this – what we've been through, how we've

come back together, what we're doing now running off to Vegas, but more important – what you're saying to me right here, right now. This is..."

"Love. Real love. Anything less wouldn't be fair to either of us, Lindsay."

LINDSAY

No one tells you that moments like this even exist. I can't imagine Daddy and Mom talking to each other this way. None of the movies and television shows I watch have couples doing this. Going so deep you touch the bottom of the emotional pool, hoping you can hold your breath long enough to come up for air.

It's intense and painful, authentic and hopeful. If he means it – truly means it – then I'm the luckiest woman in the world.

Really.

Because what man talks like this?

"I want to marry you," I say slowly, my thoughts falling in line with my mouth, "because I've loved you since we met when I was in high school. And I don't care about beating Mom and Daddy at their own game, or making you my next of kin. Those are bonuses."

His lopsided smile makes me want to kiss him again. My shoulder screams when I twist in a funny way. I gasp from the sudden pain. He frowns.

"You okay?"

"Just pulled something in my shoulder."

"Let's get to Vegas. Get the license. Find a chapel. And get you to bed." He clears his throat with meaning. "To rest."

I laugh. All the earlier churning inside, the worry and the flashbacks that plagued me when I thought about being intimate with Drew, have somehow faded. They're not one-hundred percent gone. They're not. And yet, they have less power.

They're less immediate.

Drew is safe. More than safe. In the unbridled

comfort of his words, his actions, his unwavering commitment to me, he's creating a space for me to unfurl.

I'm grateful.

And I'm responding.

As we pull back onto the highway, Drew's phone buzzes. He grabs it and answers, pulling it to his ear. Then, as if second-guessing himself, he puts it on the console and presses speakerphone.

"Hey Gentian. You're on speaker."

"Oh, uh, hi Lindsay."

"Hi Silas!"

"What's up?"

"Your cover story is starting to slip. Mrs. Bosworth is upset that Lindsay didn't invite her to the shopping trip you told them you were taking her on. Says she should have been consulted when it comes to selecting outfits for Lindsay's potential public appearances."

"Translation," I say. "Mom has nothing better to do and is pissed I skipped out on my psych eval."

Silas coughs into the phone and says, "You said it, Lindsay. Not me."

Drew should laugh, but he doesn't. Instead, he speeds up slightly, pushing the speed limit.

"Stall as much as you can. We need about three more hours. Two to get there, one to get the license and get married," Drew tells Silas.

"Got it. I'll do my best."

Click.

"Really? It only takes an hour to get the license and get married?"

"If the line isn't long. Half an hour to get the license, then go find a chapel."

"Will Elvis marry us?"

"You want that?"

"Could you imagine the look on Mom's face if I show up with wedding pictures with Elvis as the minister?" I can't stop laughing at the idea, giggling so hard my bruised ribs start to hurt.

Drew laughs, a deep rumbling of amusement. "That

makes me want to do it."

"Do they have Elvis drive-thru chapels? Kill two birds with one stone?"

Drew grabs my hand. "It's good to laugh with you."

"So that's a yes? Drive-thru chapel with Elvis?"

"Anything you want, baby. Anything you want."

CHAPTER NINETEEN

DREW

In our one and only wedding photo, Lindsay and I are in the backseat of a pink Cadillac, with Elvis at the wheel.

When we get back home, I'll have it framed and it will sit in a place of honor on our mantel. For now, it rests on my phone in digital form, ready.

Getting the license, going to the chapel, finding the place with an Elvis impersonator was easy. Kitschy and fun as we rushed to beat the clock.

And then the true spiritual moment happened. I don't remember what we said to each other, but until the day I die, I'll remember how Lindsay looked at me. A cord, a line, a tightrope stretched between us, reaching back to the past and extending forward to the future, connecting our two lives into one.

I didn't think I could love her more.

I was wrong.

While I could have done without Elvis crooning "Love Me Tender" in the background as Lindsay and I said our vows, when all was said and done, it was a fine wedding.

Lindsay is now Mrs. Andrew Foster.

I'm her husband.

And we're about to *not* have sex on our wedding night.

"Where are we staying?" she asks as we drive to the Strip. I pull into a private garage, tires squealing on the painted concrete floor. I slow down.

"I booked us a room under an assumed name." I

point to the hotel's sign.

She laughs. "Mom thinks this place is gaudy and tacky. Perfect!" I'm not sure how Monica got "gaudy" from the most expensive hotel in the Las Vegas Strip. Then again, Lindsay's mother lives in a world of her own making.

Thank God her daughter is in Realityland, where I can be with her 24/7.

I chose this place with some hesitation. It's big and glitzy, with people watchers everywhere. On the other hand, the resort is accustomed to hiding celebrities. Security in this hotel has a protocol. We're Will and Helen Jones from Tulsa, Oklahoma.

It doesn't hurt that one of the assistant directors of security was in my unit in Afghanistan on my first tour.

The private elevator takes us straight to our suite. I reserved the best I could get on short notice. A woman like Lindsay won't notice. When you're raised with money and power, you only notice what's not there. I'm pretty sure she wouldn't care if I took her to a campground or a no-tell motel. She's been through so much. She's still shaky on the inside. Sticking to what she knows – and giving her the luxury I want to give her – is the safer choice.

Making Lindsay safe is my lifelong job. Her physical safety is assured.

Time to work on the emotional side.

"I ordered room service. I figured we'd be starving by now."

"We wouldn't be hungry if you'd agreed with my idea," she teases as she gently sits on the edge of the bed, wincing and rubbing her bad elbow.

"Even I have limits, Lindsay, and having Elvis drive us to McDonald's for a wedding meal in the drive-thru wasn't going to cut it. Besides, you know we have to avoid surveillance cameras."

"Right."

Tap tap tap.

She looks at the door, then at me. I shrug.

"You are a well-oiled machine," she marvels.

The image of a well-oiled Lindsay triggers something in me. I walk quickly to the door, hyperaware that she's on a bed, we're in a location where we have all the privacy in the world, and she's my *wife*. As I tip the staff person and roll the table-cart into the room, I give myself permission to feel the never-ending passion I've felt for her all along, but kept in check.

Out of respect.

Out of a sense of knowing she needs time.

But damn it, if she keeps looking at me with those sweet bedroom eyes, I'm not sure I can hold off much longer. I don't want to scare her, or make her feel like she needs to have sex before she's ready. I don't. But she's given me more and more reasons to want her as she peels back all the walls, one by one, on this trip.

She's a feast of love.

And I'm a starving man.

"Is there anything on the menu you didn't order?" she jokes as I reveal all the dishes, one by one.

"They had fried alligator, but I thought that was a bit too much."

She smiles at me. A yawn catches her unaware, her face stretching, neck creamy and long, marred by small, healing scratches and a bruise that bisects. It's where John's arm nearly crushed her windpipe. Three or four images from that horrible day power up my internal adrenaline, making my skin crawl.

If I can have moments like this, where my body reacts to my own memory, what is Lindsay's hour-by-hour existence like?

I watch her dip lobster in melted butter. She stuffs a piece carefully in her mouth, avoiding the healing split in her lower lip, then groans with pleasure.

Damn it.

This is having a physical effect on me.

And then I realize it's okay.

It's fine.

It *should*.

She's my wife. The love of my life. We're done running. We're done fighting off the demons of the past. We literally killed them, one by one.

Together.

Now it's time to *live*.

I grab my own lobster tail and dig in.

The only taste better than this is Lindsay.

LINDSAY

I eat all the things. I do. I just keep eating and tasting. I'm stalling.

Not like stalling when I was kidnapped. Back then, I stalled to give Drew time to find me.

Now I'm stalling to avoid giving Drew time to touch me.

This is so stupid. I feel encased in cotton, my stomach exploding from cheesecake topped with blueberry compote.

Drew yawns, stretching like a man whose blood has been pooled for too long, needing to move and race, heat his body and give him relief. We're more relaxed with each other than we've been since I came home from the Island.

We're also tense as hell, because we know what should happen next.

We hold two realities at the same time. When I do that with other people, it feels surreal. When I do it with Drew, it feels true. You can have conflicting emotions about something and not have to pick one or the other. Both are part of who you are.

So I can want Drew at the same time that I'm afraid of my own reactions, afraid to be bombarded by too many memories – physical reactions – from what happened with Stellan, John and Blaine.

I'm starting to think that the only way out is through. Through *Drew*.

"Bath?"

His one-word question makes me jump slightly. I'm

174

deep in my own thoughts. He's staring at me intently, halfway between me and the bathroom. If he keeps looking at me with that smoldering gaze, then the parts of me that are still lingering, wandering behind the others in some strange, distant land, are going to quickly catch up.

"A bath? Sounds heavenly." I hear the shake in my words. As I stand I groan, my stomach full of goodness.

His phone buzzes. So does mine, simultaneously.

"Ignore it," he says, voice neutral.

"But -- "

"Silas has strict orders. No calls for me. I have my emergency phone if it's life-or-death. Those aren't." He crosses the room and puts his hands on my shoulders, rubbing them slightly, his thumbs moving in seductive circles that stoke a fire in me. "Let's take a bath."

"Together?"

He bites his lower lip, then frowns. "Or alone, if you want."

"No, no!" I stammer. "We can, together." I look at my sling. "I just don't know..."

"Wait till you see the tub. I requested one with an accessible door."

"A bathtub with a *door*?"

He motions toward the bathroom. When we walk in, I see.

Drew has truly taken care of *all* the details.

The bathtub is enormous, and taller than usual. It has seats in it on opposite ends, and a small door that he opens with a flourish.

"This is a bathtub for old people," I say, chuckling.

"We'll be old people someday," he says with a shrug. "And we'll do it together."

I try to imagine him with silver strands in his brown hair, with age lines (never wrinkles, Mom says – just age lines...) and that older, sophisticated look men acquire. He is my husband.

Mine.

Forever.

A rush of desire overwhelms me, plucking my breath,

making me ache for him in a way I didn't think I could feel ever again. It's all coming back now. My diamond ring sparkles in the low light of the room as Drew pulls me into his embrace, whispering in my ear.

"If this is too much, say so."

"It's too much," I say, "but I love it. I love you."

He kisses me, searching and sweet, then bold and strong. Every embrace is at an angle, my arm a third wheel in our relationship. As the kiss ends, he reaches for my shirt, unbuttoning the front buttons, working carefully.

"Can I help you undress?"

"Yes." I'm not shy, to my surprise. Just skittish, a little cold, and covered with aching reminders of what happened to my poor body. Once he has me fully undressed, he motions for me to sit inside the bathtub on one side, then he quickly makes himself nude, climbing in to the other seat, turning on the faucet.

"We sit in here and it fills up around us?" I marvel. He grabs a hotel-provided container of bubble bath. Sickly-sweet vanilla scent fills the air, bubbles foaming instantly in the shallow water at our feet.

"Yes. We just wait. As the water rises, our bodies acclimate, and then we enjoy. Like foreplay," he jokes, but there's no smile on his face.

Just desire.

Within minutes, the water is up to my breasts, threatening to get my shoulder wet, so he cuts off the flow. My breasts bob in the bubbles, the feeling of soaking divine. I've only taken showers with plastic bags all over my arm, so a bath is a piece of heaven.

A bath with Drew is even better.

"Drew?"

"Yeah?"

"What if I changed my mind?"

"You did?"

"Well, what if?"

"You can do that. You have all the control."

"Actually, *you* changed my mind."

"I did? How?"

"I don't know."

"Oh, come on, Lindsay. You have to tell me so I can do more of it."

"I really don't know. You didn't do it on purpose. You just...did."

"This is really unfair."

"Why? Oh! Oh, I mean, if you're not interested..."

"Oh, I'm interested. Trust me, baby. I'm interested. I just want to know what I said to make you change your mind." His toe finds mine under the water. He brushes it lightly, all along my calf, to my knee, then gently up my thigh, halfway, until I shiver.

"It wasn't one thing. I can't explain it. You just...well, you were just you."

"And being me made you..." He moves swiftly across the water, bent before me, face to face. His hands are on my thighs, waiting.

"Want *you*."

"Oh. Damn, Lindsay," he says as he sighs. "That may be the most honest thing I've ever heard."

"I think that one time I called you an asshole I was more honest."

"Hey!"

"You told me to give you the whole me." Using my one good arm, I spread it wide in a boasting gesture. "This is it." My bad elbow slips and almost dips into the water, but I save myself.

"I didn't know name calling would be part of it."

I give him a coy smile.

"What name do you have for this?" His fingers creep slowly up my side, making me relax, making me close my eyes and tip my head back, accepting his touch. He cups one breast, not moving once he has it in his hand. Just feeling, exploring, touching.

Taking his time.

I'm surprised by how much I want him. Back in the hospital, I'd given up on ever being close to anyone again. That sense of being so dirty and used, turned into an animal, a device, an object moved around my other people to meet their goals made me want to crawl into a hole and just live the rest of my life alone.

Drew wouldn't let me do that. And now here he is, loving all the pieces of me until they work together again, as one.

Helping me to be whole.

Desire lives inside his gentle touch, his intent clear. The hot bath is both soothing and cleansing, invigorating and sensual.

So is he.

"Lindsay," he whispers, moving close, his mouth against my ear, kissing me lightly on the soft skin beneath my earlobe. "You're my wife now."

I shiver at the word *wife*.

"You're mine. No one else's. I've spent all these years trying to find my way back to you. No one will ever keep us apart. No one. Do you hear me?" He looks into my eyes, dark and firm.

"I do."

"Good." His body rises up out of the water, sliding against mine. My nipples tingle and pinpoint as his chest hair, wet and flat against his pecs, rubs along my skin. He drips on my good arm as he stands before me.

I'm eye level with his naked torso.

I take my time looking.

He lets me.

In that space, I let my emotions come without judgment, my body responding to the pure sexual rawness of his naked body so close, so wet, so obviously aroused for me. Drew doesn't make a move, his taut muscles rippling with compact energy, defining a body made for protection.

Made for *me*.

How can I not want him? How can I not want him to make love to me? My thumb worries the thin gold band of my ring.

I'm scared.

I'm scared and stuck with the muscle memory of stress and terror.

It's time to replace it all, though.

Time to let love live in my bones and muscles, in my tendons and vocal cords, to replace all the dominant worry with a force stronger than hate.

With Drew's love.

Our love.

For four years my entire world was the Island. Schedules and routines, confessions and pills, the conspicuous putting back together of the pieces of me the world saw.

My inner life didn't matter.

I protected it like a secret treasure.

As I stand, the residual bubbles clinging to my thighs and belly, Drew gives me a long look, taking his time, too. There is no pretense. The room smells like vanilla as I inhale deeply, blurting out the first true feeling that comes to mind.

"I shouldn't want you," I say, touching his bare chest, my palm scraping against his wet nipple, his eyes turning soft as he tries to understand. I step into his embrace, my sling in the way. Our thighs meet and I can feel how much he wants me.

"What?"

"I – shouldn't want you this much. It's so overpowering. It's all I can think about now."

"Why shouldn't you? You can feel whatever you want, baby." His hands are strong on my good shoulder, my hip, then up my back, feeling me, bringing me here and now, pulling me in from the wide distance where I've been living for too long, out on the edges.

"I'm in a million little parts, scattered to the winds, trying to collect them all and put them back together again."

He kisses my bad shoulder, then my neck, my cheek, my nose. "Every kiss is a piece of you coming home," Drew whispers. "How many kisses do you need?"

"All of them."

"I have more than enough to bring back all the shattered pieces of you, Lindsay. You get all my kisses,

179

forever," he says, and then he stops talking, mouth on mine.

The warm, wet heat of his body makes me feel more grounded, his tongue slipping in to tell me all the ways I can be close to him. I only have one hand, my movements drawn down, wanting to find his solid muscle, marveling at the hard lines of his body. Drew is kissing me with the quiet urgency of a man who is holding back for reasons of honor, of respect.

I don't want that.

I want him to make love to me with wild abandon, with the synergy of two people who find refuge in letting go.

CHAPTER TWENTY

DREW

I really was prepared to spend our wedding night celibate. I was. If that's what she wanted, I was prepared. Stilling my desire was hard, but I'm accustomed to meeting challenges.

Lindsay's change of heart is an honor. It's a sign of trust, of commitment. I've served her well if she can feel passion and excitement, crave intimacy and caring.

I have to do this right.

I have to make it so good for her.

Steam surrounds us, left over from the bath, making her skin dewey and her eyes so big and round, pleading with me to touch her everywhere, kiss away the hurt, make her remember what it's like to be loved and wanted with an all-consuming need that she's the center of everything, of the world, of my universe.

She's damn close to being holy, a goddess, an altar for me to worship. Maybe my kisses are enough. My hands, rough from work and years of field exercises, feel so unworthy of her flesh as she matches me, touch for touch, sound for sound, breath for breath.

We step out of the bathtub and I reach for a towel, thick and abundant, drying the ends of her hair, patting her back, her shoulders, her arms, then sliding over her breasts, belly, ass, and legs with the attentive care of a man who can't get enough.

"Drew," she whispers, like moonlight spins itself from her heart and comes out through her mouth. The rush of my name from Lindsay makes my heart beat double time.

We've had sex twice since she came home, my body fully inside hers, once reverent, once playful and fast, speedy and insistent.

This time she is my *wife*. We are connected by choice, by law.

They say that an orgasm is a little death. If that's true, then what is the resurrection? We come back to each other after the divine, after relinquishing our bodies, our blood, to the mad rush of climax. We bond over shared flesh, by opening ourselves to each other, by saying I do.

As I lead her to the bed by her good hand, help her under the covers, then prowl up her sweet, fine body, her curves tight and bruises lessening, I find myself wanting to die a thousand times while inside her.

And only her.

"You lead the way," I say softly, breathing hard, practically shaking from holding back. Part of me wants to kiss her, slide into her, ride hard and make her moan until she goes hoarse from pleasure, until all her fear has been fucked out of her, until we're both boneless and nothing but our bodies and mutual pleasure exists.

That's her call, though.

The other part knows she needs a tender touch to tease her out of the remaining fear that lingers on her skin, a tight, taut feeling that is tangible. I give her a long, languid kiss, wet and slow, waiting for her cues. When she starts to squirm under me, moving her legs so she's pressed against my thigh, rubbing against me with a rhythm as she turns breathless, I know what to do next.

"My shoulder," she gasps. "How can we do this? I'm -- " She laughs as if this is crazy, as if her gunshot wound is her fault. As if she's embarrassed by it.

"We'll do it," I respond, moving down her body, brushing kisses on her nipples. "Between your shoulder and my broken finger, we both have to adjust." I continue kissing her in the fine valley between her breasts, down her creamy belly, then finally where she tastes like wordless nirvana.

I open her and she widens for me, urging with little sighs and her fingers in my hair. The pure joy of being invited to do this makes me rock hard. I want her so much. She wiggles, her body taking on a rhythm I follow, her voice begging as she says my name with increasing fervor.

My good hand slides under her, cupping her ass as my face and tongue move in whatever way I need to give her this. She deserves all the pleasure I can create, and I want her to take until she's sated.

Abruptly, she stops me, her hand fisting my hair and pulling up. Our eyes meet and she is blazing, fired up with passion and trembling. She breathes hard, each exhale loud and hot.

Then she says,

"Let's make this official. I want you in me, and I want you to make love to me. Please, Drew. Please. I want to come with you inside me. I want you more than I thought I could."

LINDSAY

"I will. Just wait," he whispers, one hand on my breast, his thumb and index finger curling around my nipple, the taped pinkie finger hard and strange, but endearing. His other hand moves between my legs and oh! *Oh!*

He slips a finger inside me, three sensations all combining at one. Breast, clit, and finger all work together in a choreographed way as all my thoughts dissolve, my body moving in whatever way it needs to seek more pleasure.

And then he licks me until I see heaven explode, his attentions so urgent, so determined to give me pleasure that I have to submit, have to give in, have to trust and release and thrust and lose myself in him.

I'm moaning his name, biting the end of my pillow, making sounds I didn't know I could make, seeing colors that surely don't exist anywhere but here as Drew drives home again and again that I am enough, that I count, too, that I deserve this and that he deserves me. He moves to make me confront my own ecstasy, not letting me avoid the orgasms, and then I explode again, as if the first time was just practice.

I go cold and numb, burn and feel everything, my exquisite ride along his tongue so dirty, so filthy, so perfect.

And then he's kissing me, hard and loose, his mouth lingering with my taste, his hands everywhere, nowhere, and I have never wanted anyone to be between my legs so desperately as I want him now.

As he starts to enter me, my shoulder screams and I gasp, then cry out from panic.

"Wait," he says, gently moving me over, pulling out. "You be on top. Sit up. ride me, Lindsay. Ride me." His eyes flash with erotic anticipation as I awkwardly trade places with him, our bodies slick and sweaty, until I'm on top of him, my thighs against his, my legs open and my good hand holding on to his abs for balance. As I slide down over him I suck in my breath, Drew imitating me.

My diamond glitters in the darkness, shining in the moonlight, splayed across his belly button, a reminder. All the rolling muscle of his torso moves like a pond rippling as a stone is thrown in, his body working hard to thrust up and catch me, his ass tightening with each wave.

"Lindsay, you feel so good. So hot. Oh," he rasps as we move together, trying to find the right speed, the right angle.

I feel a keening deep within, a spark of recognition as he moves inside, with each thrust, each shift, each growing layer of love. The screams of demons and tormenters inside make way for cries of ecstasy as Drew's soul warms the dark corners of my own. My body is exposed for him, my sling bulky and in the way, but it's all right.

This is real. This is real love.

This is real lovemaking.

He reaches up and squeezes both breasts at the same time, then skims my skin with his rough hands, finding my hips, grinding me into him, making me move just enough until my clit is in a new position, the extra friction wet and perfect against him. An orgasm starts in the core of my belly, riding through my lower body, rising up to the hollow of my throat, spreading to my nipples, my tongue, my back and shoulders. It takes over like a spirit animal soaring over sacred ground, riding over the plains in twilight, seeking truth.

"I love you," Drew groan. "I'm about to -- " He goes rigid, then moves fast, groans deep and resounding, a vibration that adds to my pleasure. I tip, too and struggle for balance as I lose all sense of my body in space and time, clinging to him, later leaving small marks on his belly with my fingernails. I tell myself I'll kiss them when this is over, greedy for the intoxicating rush of orgasm, reveling in his body and mine using each other with so much trust and love.

"Drew, I can't, I can't stop, I -- "

"Don't, baby. Don't stop. Go. I'll be here when you come back. Right here," he says, reaching down between us, his thumb stroking the spot where I need him most, my body rising high, a thin cry making lightning shoot through me, Drew's other hand on my hip, pinning me in place with a near-brutal rhythm that makes me come and come and come until I can't even ask him to stop. I am shaking and crying but it's good, so good.

So *Drew*.

I fall forward, slumped on his body, my ass in the air and my torso curled in a weird way as I protect my shoulder. He's panting, too, and feels like all the marbled muscle in him has gone still. My hair covers the fine grooves of his ribs, his skin shining with a sheen from exertion, and as I rest on top of him, I realize it's this – the shared recovery after the unraveling – that makes for connection.

We aren't intimate because we find other people attractive.

We find other people attractive because they choose to be intimate and share their soft underbellies.

He plays with a piece of my hair, stroking it from my neck, his words hard to hear as he says, "We've been to hell and back."

"Yes." I sit up. He moves quickly, helping me to settle down, supporting my arm so it doesn't hurt. Then he rests next to me, pulling up the warm covers, burrowing in. I've been holding my body and breath, tense with aftershocks from sex, and I release.

I relax into him.

"That was the best sex we've ever had as husband and wife," he says with a smile in his voice.

"Oh, c'mon," I tease. "We can do better than that."

"Next time."

"Promise?" I yawn, the day hitting me at once, my eyes unbearably sleepy, lids impossible to hold up.

"Yes," he says, kissing my temple. "Are you happy?"

"Completely."

"Satisfied?" His hand finds my thigh.

"Fully. In every way possible," I insist, laughing.

"Then I did my job."

We're out in seconds.

We don't dream.

CHAPTER TWENTY-ONE

LINDSAY

The gentle tap on the door seems too timid for a true emergency. I'm naked, we're sticky, and my mouth is dry, like someone blotted all the moisture out. Forgetting momentarily about my broken shoulder, I start to sit up, then let out a tiny scream.

Drew is off the bed, feet on the floor, hand on his gun in under a second. He holds it pointing down, but every muscle in his naked body is flexed, ready to act.

"What? What's wrong?" He's so *precise*. It's shocking. As he scans the room, he's so serious, so deadly, the laugh dies in my throat.

Drew stretches up, body honed in on the hotel room door, where someone on the other side says, "Drew? It's Adam. We have a situation."

"Who's Adam?" I ask as Drew shoves his feet into his suit pants, skipping underwear, buttoning the pants but not bothering with the belt.

"Old buddy," he says as he marches to the door, gun tucked into the waistband of the pants. I almost laugh, because it looks so weird, right there above his hot, hard ass.

The door opens. I sit up, feeling exposed and vulnerable, my shoulder such an obstacle. The two have a conversation in low voices, then Drew says *thank you*, closes the door, and comes into the room.

Holding an iPad.

"Your parents are waiting to FaceTime with us, Lindsay," he says.

I point to the iPad with my good hand. "You mean *now*?"

He shakes his head slowly. "Yeah. Gentian tried, but apparently Harry figured it all out pretty quickly. Someone at the license bureau knew who you were and called him, wanting money to hold off on going public. You know how it works." He's cynical. He should be.

I *do* know how this works.

"My parents are *live* on that?" I point to the iPad.

"Yeah. I've got them muted."

"Oh, Mom must be flipping out."

He turns the screen to me. I pull the covers up, making sure I'm decent. Mom is screaming at the screen, her perfectly-coiffed blonde head like staring at a cream-colored snowball on fire. She's in a red rage.

I can't help it.

I start laughing.

Drew sets the tablet on the nightstand, face down. "Let's get ourselves set up," he says, offering me a few pillows as I sit up. "Do you want a shirt?" he asks as I settle in, propping up my slung arm on an extra pillow.

"No," I respond, pulling the covers over my breasts, tucking the sheet under my arms. "Screw it. Screw them." I hold out my ringed hand and he takes it. He's wearing a simple gold band the Elvis impersonator sold us for fifty bucks. I like how our hands look together.

"Okay." He looks at his own unclothed chest. The light smattering of hair across his pecs is just enough to make me want to touch him, to feel it tickle my palm. I hold back. His bruises are fading, like mine, but they tell a story.

They're memory in the body, stored until it can heal. Then the memory moves on, living solely in the mind.

"Ready?" He asks. We're next to each other, on the bed. Drew turned on the nightstand lights. We hold hands. He takes his knees and props them up, placing the tablet on them.

"Ready."

He hits unmute.

" -- you are crazy! Lindsay, you get right back here now. This makes it abundantly clear that you need psychiatric help! Who runs off and gets married like this? Only an unstable, traumatized woman who has been manipulated by her -- "

"Hi Mom!" I chirp, waving with my good hand, moving slowly so she sees the rings. "Thank you so much for your blessing." I grin, nice and wide, ignoring my split lip.

Drew giggles.

Giggles.

"Do you have any idea what this is going to look like when the press gets wind of it? Drew was just painted as your unstable ex-boyfriend who stalked you after your father made the error of hiring him for you security team! The press is still getting all the details wrong, and -- "

"Monica." Daddy's in the room, I see, behind Mom's fiery head. "Monica, let someone else speak."

"Like who? Lindsay's babbling nonsense and pretending her betrayal is just fine. My God, Harry, this is a PR nightmare! The only reason someone would run off and get married in Vegas – VEGAS – like this is if they're crazy, or if they – OH MY GOD!" Mom moans, swooning. "You didn't *have* to get married, did you?"

"What does that mean?" Drew asks.

"LINDSAY!" Mom screams. "ARE YOU PREGNANT? DID YOU RUN OFF AND GET MARRIED BECAUSE YOU HAD TO? BECAUSE THAT WOULD EXPLAIN SO MUCH."

I'm dumbfounded.

Mom had robbed me of speech.

Daddy's face appears as Mom recedes, mumbling to herself. I see they're in Daddy's office at The Grove, to-go trays littering the small table by his desk. He looks haggard and tired.

"Sweetie, are you? Pregnant?" he asks.

"No," I answer honestly. "I'm not." I open my mouth to mention that I've been home from the Island for barely three weeks, so how in the hell could I be pregnant?

Mom appears again, edging Daddy out. "Well, thank GOD -- "

Drew pulls me close. In the tiny little window on the screen, I see how we appear to them. Drew's shirtless, my shoulders are bare other than the covers up to my armpits. I have a raging case of sex bedhead. Drew grins like a fiend.

He kisses my cheek. "But we can get right on that, Monica! Thanks for the suggestion!"

Mom looks flustered. "Get right on what?"

"You seem really eager for us to start producing grandchildren for you." He looks at me with wide, joking eyes. "Can you imagine 'Grandma Monica'?"

"Oh, I can imagine it, all right," I choke back.

"Harry! Harry! Say something to them! Dear God, Harry, I'm too young to be a grandmother. And besides, if you're going to time a grandchild during an election, there's a protocol for this. For maximum positive press, you need to..."

Mom's voice fades out as Daddy looks at the screen, deadpan, shaking his head.

Drew leans toward me and whispers, "I can turn this off whenever you want."

"No. It's okay." I smile at Daddy, who smiles back, his eyes full of love.

"We can get this sham marriage annulled!" Mom shouts in the background. "We can undo this! For God's sakes, Harry, step in! Don't you have anything to say to Drew?"

One corner of Daddy's mouth tips up, and he looks at me, then Drew, eyes narrowing as he stops and really studies my new husband.

"What do you want me to say, Monica?" he asks in a weary voice, giving her an epic eye roll only we can see.

"Something to fix this!" she shoots back.

Daddy smiles, fixated on Drew, who stares back, matching him, unwavering.

And then my father says:
"Welcome to the family, son."

THE END

ABOUT THE AUTHOR

Meli Raine writes romantic suspense with hot bikers, intense undercover DEA agents, bad boys turned good, and Special Ops heroes -- and the women who love them.

Meli rode her first motorcycle when she was five years old, but she played in the ocean long before that. She lives in New England with her family.

Visit her on Facebook at
http://www.facebook.com/meliraine

Join her New Releases and Sales newsletter at:
http://eepurl.com/beV0gf

She also writes romantic comedy as Julia Kent, and is half of the co-authoring team for the Diana Seere paranormal shifter romance books.

OTHER BOOKS BY MELI RAINE

Suggested Reading Order

The Breaking Away Series
Finding Allie
Chasing Allie
Keeping Allie

The Coming Home Series
RETURN
REVENGE
REUNION

The Harmless Series
A Harmless Little Game
A Harmless Little Ruse
A Harmless Little Plan

22562933R00116

Printed in Great Britain
by Amazon